Spellbinding

MAYA GOLD

MIDDLE SCHOOL

Point

Library of Congress Cataloging-in-Publication Data

Gold, Maya.
Spellbinding / Maya Gold.
p. cm.
Summary: When sixteen-year-old Abby traces her deceased mother's family to the Salem Witch Trials, the nightmares she has been having begin to make sense, but soon she is caught up in a love triangle and an age-old quest for revenge.
ISBN 978-0-545-43380-8
[1. Witchcraft — Fiction. 2. High schools — Fiction. 3. Schools — Fiction. 4. Dating (Social customs) — Fiction. 5. Revenge — Fiction. 6. Salem (Mass.) — History — Colonial period, ca. 1600-1775 — Fiction. 7. Massachusetts — Fiction.] I. Title.
PZ7.G5628Spe 2013
[Fic] — dc23
2012016692

12 11 10 9 8 7 6 5 4 3   13 14 15 16 17 18/0

Printed in the U.S.A.   40
First printing, April 2013

For my magical niece Emily

Prologue

THE GIRLS SHRIEK AND WRITHE ON THE
floor of the metinghouse, tearing their hair, their white
aprons. Their screams are unearthly, like night sounds of prey
as an owl swoops down, talons ripping through flesh as it carries some helpless thing off to its death. But the girls are alive,
fully alive, and whatever is tearing at them can't be seen.

The room is shadowy, lit by firelight and guttering candles. Hard wooden benches, a sour odor of fear. The men wear
dark clothing. They mutter and frown, passing judgment.

A woman leaps to her feet, wild-eyed. "She put a curse on
my daughter!" she cries.

She's pointing directly at me.

The ground seems to shift underneath my feet. There's a
swirling through darkness, and suddenly I am outdoors. Dusty
planks turn into mud, rutted by wagon wheels, littered with
straw. My wrists chafe in ropes. My hair has been hacked off

with shears, and my scalp feels raw and exposed. I'm ashamed of the way I must look, like a badly peeled egg. Torches flicker around me as townspeople poke me with sticks, kick at my hobbled ankles. When I lift my head, they draw back in fear. I hear the words "evil," "accursed." I hear someone hiss, "Die, witch!" They are talking about me, spreading lies.

The mob jostles me toward a stone bridge, where a creek widens into a pond. Its edges are muddy, surrounded by cattails and slime. I think of the things that might live in there — muskrats, water snakes, frogs — and my skin crawls. "Let us prove her guilt. Throw her in!" cries a man, and the crowd takes up the chant. "Throw her in, throw her in!"

The torchlight distorts their faces. They look like masks, angry and brutal. Only one person stands apart — a young man. In the slash of light flickering over his handsome face, I notice that one of his striking green eyes is split by a wedge of bright blue. He's looking right at me, and for a second I feel I can hear his unspoken thoughts.

We shall be together. No fear.

And then everything's water. I'm thrown through the surface. My body is surrounded by dark, icy water, above and below me. It soaks my heavy skirts, pulling me under. With hands and feet bound, I flail and thrash as the cold liquid fills my mouth and throat, sucking me down to the bottom. To death.

My eyes are wide open. Above me, a black fringe of tree-tops rims the night sky. Is the boy with the green-and-blue eyes still up there somewhere? His words echo inside my head. We shall be together. *How? How can I not fear?* Help me, *I think.* Whoever you are, come and get me.

My lungs burn. My limbs feel so heavy. I stare up at the full moon through water, deep water, struggling to reach him, unable to breathe. . . .

Chapter 1

I BOLT UPRIGHT, WIDE-EYED AND GASPING. I try to shake that vision out of my head. I'm *not* at the bottom of a dark pond, unable to get to the surface, lungs ready to burst. I'm on a bright yellow school bus, which has just parked outside my *other* nightmare, Ipswich High School. This is real life, hello.

But I've still got goose bumps. I can't believe I fell asleep on the bus and had one of *those* dreams. It's bad enough waking up from a nightmare in my own bedroom, with birds doing their morning warbles and sun pouring over the little-girl wallpaper I can't bear to change because my mom picked it out. But freaking out on the *school bus*? Not cool.

I glance around, feeling self-conscious. Luckily, my bus is half-empty this year, so no one sits next to me, ever. And the few kids around me are too busy grabbing their backpacks to notice I just woke up looking like some sort of special effect.

Breathe, Abby. I pick up my shoulder bag, straighten my books into a neat stack, and head down the aisle to the door. My head's pounding as if I'm a bass drum, instead of a high school junior with too much on her mind (says my dad), with tension headaches (says the school nurse), or just born to be weird (says me).

Weird isn't even the word. Being weird takes confidence. Makayla Graf, the art student with turquoise-streaked hair and six cartilage posts in one ear, is weird. So is Samson Hobby, the Goth boy who wears a black skirt with his biker boots. They stand out in a crowd, and everybody at Ipswich High knows who they are. I'm just background. A frizzy blonde head sticking up in the tall-kid back row of class photos, a name on school newsletter lists: Abigail Silva, National Honor Society. Abigail Silva, Science Fair silver medalist.

Abby Silva: invisible.

If I had to pick a distinguishing mark, something to make me not boringly normal, it wouldn't be nightmares and spike headaches. But ever since I turned sixteen, I've been having them more and more often. It scares me. I'm starting to worry I might be bipolar, or heading toward some kind of breakdown. It feels like my skin isn't doing its job, like too much sensation gets in all the time. Everything scrapes on my senses like sandpaper. Maybe this is the flip side of being invisible: Nobody sees me, but I notice *everything*.

The parking lot looks like a mass migration of kids, all carrying backpacks and wearing some variation of jeans and T-shirts. It reminds me of a film they showed us in freshman biology, about salmon moving upstream to spawn. The stream widens out as I get through the tunnel of buses and reach the section where kids with cars park.

There's nothing on earth I want more than a car of my own. A car is like oxygen. It means freedom, autonomy, getting to go where you want, when you want. I've had my driver's permit for six long months, and I'm finally taking my road test *tomorrow*. My friend Rachel Mendoza is driving me to the test site. Rachel's a senior, and she got her license last year. In fact, there she is now, getting out of her sensible navy blue Volvo.

That car is so Rachel. Rachel's parents both play in the Boston Symphony. She got her glossy black hair from her Venezuelan-born father, her wide-set gray eyes from her Irish-American mother, and her musical talent from both — she plays the cello beautifully. She's polite, hardworking, and totally brilliant — she's been tutoring me after school for my trigonometry class. All in all, she's the kind of girl that makes parents say to their kids, "Why can't you be more like Rachel?"

Rachel is currently the only person in Ipswich, Massachusetts, who actually goes out of her way to hang out with me. I'm not one of those misfit, avoid-at-all-costs kids, but there's been a big hole in my social life ever since my best friend Valerie moved to Sarasota last summer. Valerie and I texted and Skyped nonstop for the first few months, but then Valerie found other friends, then another best friend, and I felt — well, sort of abandoned. Till Rachel. She's going to Vassar in the fall, and I don't know how I'm going to get through my last year of high school without her.

I wave, heading toward her. Rachel gives me a little hug and smile that almost erases the leftover dread from my drowning nightmare. "Hey, love those earrings," she says.

My hands go to my earlobes. What did I put on in the pre-school bus rush? Oh, right. The turquoise dangles Rachel gave me for my sixteenth birthday, after her family went to Santa Fe on vacation.

"Good taste," I say, grinning.

Rachel opens the Volvo's back door, expertly angling her cello case out of the tight space between seats.

"Hold Igor a minute?" she asks, and I take the heavy black case, stepping backward and out of her way. Rachel likes giving names to inanimate objects. Her car is named Gimli, and her laptop, for reasons known only to Rachel, is Rubybegonia. Her cello is Igor.

Standing upright, the cello case does look a bit like a misshapen human. I drape a protective arm over its neck. As Rachel shrugs into her backpack straps, a car zooms up behind us. It's one I'd know anywhere: Travis Brown's Alfa Romeo. My whole face gets warm in an instant, and I dip my head so I won't look like a moron.

What is it that makes Travis shine like the sun? He's had that effect on me ever since we were little. I'll never forget him tying my sneakers for me on the elementary school playground, when I couldn't remember that frog-jumps-into-a-pond trick to save my life. Travis taught me the make-two-loops shortcut his big brother showed him, and I've tied my shoes that way ever since. He was a whole grade older, which seems like a lifetime in little-kid years, and my very first crush. Let's face it, I've never completely outgrown said crush, even though Travis is the textbook definition of "out of my league."

It isn't so much that he's gorgeous, though he certainly is — tall and well built, with a confident bounce in his stride, sky blue eyes, and a grin that would melt an ice-cream cone. It's more that he seems so at home in his skin, like he's never wasted a second wondering what anyone thinks about him. He just glides through his life, winning track meets and soccer games, making friends, having fun. It's all good. He's not stupid or smug, he's just happy to be who he is.

Well, who wouldn't be happy to be Travis Brown? Even his car is cool. It's a low-slung red convertible, perfect for two. And of course there are two people in it: Travis, looking dashing in his vintage Ray-Bans and blue Polo shirt, and Megan Keith. Megan might also look appealing to a stranger who didn't know that beneath that long chestnut hair, natural tan, and perfect beach body beats the heart of a poisonous snake.

How can Travis go out with her? I wonder for the umpteenth time. Travis is the hottest guy in the school, who could literally have anybody he wanted, and *that's* who he picked? It makes perfect sense on one level — Megan's the reigning queen of the popular crowd. And I've seen her on the boardwalk in the summer — she certainly knows how to rock a bikini. But isn't there more to life than eye candy? Even if you're a guy?

I hear myself sighing and send out a swift mental kick. If there's any cliché I do *not* want to be, it's the geek mooning over the popular boy. With the popular girlfriend. It's just too pathetic.

All this runs through my head as I'm standing there

like the proverbial deer caught in headlights, one arm still draped around Igor.

Travis brakes, smiling as he waits for me to move out of the way. Megan smirks at the cello case.

"Oooh. Is that your *boyfriend*?" she asks, her voice dripping with fake sweetness.

My mouth opens, but nothing comes out. I could die of embarrassment.

"Oh, get over yourself," Rachel says to Megan, grabbing Igor from me and striding past Travis's car. Somehow my feet come unstuck from the pavement, and I slink after her, hoping my ponytail frizz doesn't look like a haystack.

"Ugh." Rachel shudders as Travis parks his car. "She is odious."

Yes, she is. And incredibly lucky. I'd give anything to be sitting where she is right now.

But I've never told Rachel about my secret crush. Valerie got it — we used to spend hours dissecting my interactions with Travis. But Rachel has no use for popular jocks, so I just agree with her put-down of Megan.

"Exactly the word I was looking for," I tell her. "Thank you."

"*De nada,*" says Rachel. As we go inside, I sneak a look over my shoulder at Travis and Megan. My ears are still flaming.

Our school's pretty big, so I don't cross paths with Travis all morning. But somehow — just luck of the draw — I run into Megan outside my US History class. She's sweeping down the hall with her equally toxic friends, Amber and Sloane. Amber is a bland-faced strawberry blonde, and Sloane is thin, dark, and petite, like a mean little weasel. She actually *looks* like a weasel, with her sharp, beady eyes and permanent sneer. Neither Amber nor Sloane is what you'd call a beauty, and sometimes I wonder if Megan chose her sidekicks like bad bridesmaids' dresses, to ensure that she gets all the spotlight.

Megan whispers something to Amber and Sloane, and I hear the word *cello*. Great.

She apparently told them I'm dating a musical instrument or something, because they crack up like hyenas as soon as they see me, pretending to saw violins. What are they, third graders? But I don't say a thing. Rachel is braver than I am — I never want to go toe-to-toe with the queens of mean. I bite my lip, heading for class.

"What's the matter?" Sloane demands, stepping right in front of me. "Don't you think Megan's funny? I think she's funny, don't you, Amber?"

"Megan's *hysterical*," Amber agrees, ever the suck-up.

"Or maybe you don't think she's funny 'cause you like her boyfriend," says Sloane, her tone taking on a more threatening edge.

I can feel myself blushing, the heat rising into the tips of my ears. *How do they know? Do they know? Maybe they just assume* everybody *likes Travis.*

I open my mouth to deny it, but Megan tosses her head. "Don't waste your energy, Sloane. As if Travis would possibly look twice at *her.*" She gives me a phony smile, lazily flicking her fingers. "Buh-bye." And they're gone.

It's at moments like this when the prospect of summer vacation, just two months away, seems like heaven on earth.

Breathe, Abby. Breathe.

My US History class is taught by the toughest teacher in the whole school, Ms. Baptiste. She's African-American, and she brings fresh perspectives to studying the Civil War for what feels like the fiftieth time since first grade. We just had a unit test on Reconstruction, and as she clicks down the aisle in her purple pumps, handing back graded papers, I can hear students groan all around me.

"Everyone's brain must have been circling the maypole on this one," she says, handing me a paper with a B minus in red. My stomach sinks. "So I'm going to give you an extra assignment for Monday," Ms. Baptiste goes on. "I want everyone to bring in a detailed family tree. Trace your ancestors back to the first person who set foot on American soil."

Is she serious? Why is she loading us down with *more* homework when we're already swamped?

Branko Jankovic grins and says, "Cake." Both his parents were born in Slovenia.

But Samson Hobby frowns. "What's this got to do with the Civil War?"

Good question, I think, but as usual I keep my mouth shut.

"Plenty," says Ms. Baptiste. "One of your ancestors might have owned one of mine. History is a living thing, people. It's not just a bunch of dusty old dates. It's your own skin and blood."

She passes out sheets with a family tree template and a list of genealogy websites and resources. This actually could be exciting — I know my dad's family (my Silva side) hails from Portugal, but I don't know very much about my mom's side, other than the fact that they've been in America since the 1600s. Normally, I'd look forward to doing some digging into the past. But the thought of more pressure on top of my driving test gives me a headache.

"Let's take a good look at the mix in this classroom," Ms. Baptiste adds. "I bet we'll find plenty of history."

"And this is due *Monday*?" asks Samson, tossing his dyed blond dreadlocks indignantly. "That's, like, no notice!"

Kate Reeder and some of the other kids mumble agreement, but Ms. Baptiste doesn't back down. She says, "Deal with it."

I have to look after my kid brother, Matt, and his soccer-team buddy Kevin on Friday night, since Dad's on the evening shift at his computer store.

After I've loaded both boys up with mac and cheese (made from a package; I can't convince Kevin my home-made is better), I head up to my bedroom and go online. I figure I'd better get the genealogy project started tonight. I'm planning on making a PowerPoint for my presentation, which hopefully won't take too much time.

I start by typing in my grandparents' names to the genealogy sites Ms. Baptiste suggested. Tracking down ancestors is a little like surfing through Facebook friends: You type in one name, and a whole list comes up, and you click on the next, and the next, working your way back through the generations. It's kind of addictive — in fact, it almost feels like the video game I can hear Matt and Kevin playing downstairs. Minus the sound effects and the shouting, of course. I track down the Portuguese Silvas in no time, and then get to work on Mom's side of the family.

This takes a little more doing, because they've been here for centuries. Luckily, some distant cousin I've never met has already posted a family tree tracing her ancestry back to Ethan Dale, a foot soldier in the Revolution. That's kind of cool. But she couldn't get any further, and neither can I. Closing my eyes, I try to summon up anything Mom might have told me about her family when I did a project about the Pilgrims in fifth grade. That was right before she got sick.

Suddenly, I remember Mom saying that her uncle Ben was named after a cabin boy ancestor with the unforgettable name of Benevolence Fletcher.

I grin and type in FLETCHER, BENEVOLENCE. After a couple blind alleys, his name pops up on a ship's registry from 1636. *Bingo!* I feel a flicker of excitement. Benevolence landed in Plymouth, where he married a woman named Mercy Gilbert.

Mercy and Benevolence, whoa. What did they name their *kids*?

All too soon, I find out. Caleb, Jeremiah, Miles, William, Annabel, Silas, and Prudence. I let out a sigh.

That's a lot of descendants to trace. But it turns out that four of them died in childhood — life must have been hard in colonial times — and Silas never married. So the missing ancestor must be either Prudence or William.

Here again, I hit a dead end. Did I miss someone? I go back, retracing my steps. It's not just about doing well on this project for school, though I definitely want to override that B minus. It's also that I'm feeling more connected to Mom. I keep hearing her voice in my ear as I search for her ancestors.

But my eyes are getting tired and all the names are blurring together. The next thing I know I'm slumped over my laptop, and Dad's shaking my shoulder and telling me that it's past midnight and I need to get to bed *now*. I mumble something to him about a genealogy assignment before I stumble into bed.

Staying up late has a fringe benefit: I'm too tired to have any more of my strange nightmares. Still, I'm pretty bleary when I get down to breakfast the next day.

Mom always used to make us French toast and elaborate omelettes on weekends. I've tried to keep up that tradition — she taught me how to cook and I totally love it — but today my stomach's too nervous for anything more than Greek yogurt. Watching Matt and Kevin inhale chocolate milk with the donuts Dad bought them makes me want to hurl. I'm relieved when they leave the table and charge upstairs, looking for Matt's soccer kneepads.

This is my moment. I get up and refill Dad's coffee cup, adding sugar and half-and-half so it's just the right color.

"Thanks, Abby," he says, running a hand through his bristly dark hair and glancing up at me. My father's a good-looking guy — tan and rugged. I couldn't look any less like him. If you didn't know my blue-eyed mother when she was alive, and just saw him with me and my brother, you'd probably assume that I must be adopted.

I've got Dad's attention, a rare thing on a Saturday morning. I blurt out my question before he disappears into soccer-coach mode and forgets that I'm here. "So, remember that project I was working on late last night? I've got your family traced all the way back to Cristobal Silva, who shipped out of Lisbon in 1907. But I hit a brick wall on Mom's side."

Dad looks impatient, and I get the feeling there's something else he wants to talk to me about. Or maybe it's just that his mind's more on soccer than homework.

"Your mother's family came over from England, a couple boats after the *Mayflower*," Dad says. "Your teacher can't seriously expect you to go back four hundred years."

"Well, the thing is, I did. I found the first two genera-tions, but then there's a gap of about ninety years. Did Mom ever say anything about her ancestors?"

"Ann wouldn't have cared. She thought all that New England blue-blood stuff was nonsense. Good thing, or she'd never have married the son of a Portuguese fisher-man." Dad chugs his coffee, checking the time on his sports watch.

I know he's right. Mom was a botanist, and didn't hold stock with purebred anything, not even dogs. "Mutts make the best pets," she used to say. "Hybrid vigor." But that doesn't explain why her line disappeared altogether for almost a century.

"Ready!" says Matt, skidding into the kitchen in his green-and-gold uniform with Kevin right behind him.

Great. There go my two minutes of focus. "Dad, it's for school. She never said anything?"

Dad stands up, grabbing his coach jacket off a hook. "Nope. But one of her great-uncles took me aside at our wedding and said, 'Joe, your bride may be lovely, but she's got witch blood. They were hanging her people at Salem.'"

The hair on the back of my neck stands up. "Really?" I say at the same time as Matt says, "No way!"

"That great-uncle was a loon," says Dad. "The witch part was probably a joke, but I do think a few of her ancestors settled in Salem." He picks up a net bag of practice balls, grabs his car keys off the hook, and then he, Matt, and Kevin are gone. Not even a word of *good luck, hope you pass your driver's test*. Mom would have wished me well.

Scratch that. Mom would have taken me.

I throw the breakfast dishes into the sink. Then I take my laptop out onto the screen porch and boot it up, googling SALEM. The first thing that pops up is WITCH TRIALS, with thousands of weblinks. I click on the first one and take a deep breath as I read about the witch-hunt hysteria that gripped the Puritan village in 1692:

One of the darkest times in American history began with a false accusation by schoolgirls. Between 1692 and 1693, the village of Salem tried dozens of people on charges of practicing witchcraft. Twenty men and women were put to death; still more died in prison awaiting trial.

There's a strange pounding inside my head and I can't shake the creepy sensation that I already know what I'm reading about. But how could that be?

Salem's not far away from where I've always lived, but I haven't been there since I was a toddler. It's not on a direct route to anywhere else — you have to drive out of your way to go into the village. Mom thought the whole place was a tourist trap, especially around Halloween. So even though some of my classmates' families went there every fall, we steered clear of the whole Salem witch thing. Now I wonder why.

The names in my research swim past my eyes: Sarah Good, the mad beggar imprisoned with her four-and-a-half-year-old daughter, Dorcas . . . Tituba, the Caribbean slave who taught young girls how to tell fortunes by cracking eggs, and was accused of witchcraft when three of the girls in her charge started showing strange symptoms . . .

When I read about the afflicted girls' fits, writhing and twitching and clutching their hair, my heart starts to flutter.

It's just like my nightmare.

I don't even hear Rachel pull into the driveway. "Abby?" she calls, letting herself in the front door.

Oh, right. My driver's test. "Coming!" I yell. But as I reach over to turn off my laptop, a name on-screen catches my eye.

It's my mother's.

Chapter 2

"YOU'RE KIDDING," SAYS RACHEL AS WE drive away from my house. "Do you mean just her first name? Because there are plenty of Anns in New England."

I shake my head, still in shock. "It was her middle name," I say. "Solart. Which is much rarer. Mom told me that 'Solart' came from an old family surname. And, according to the website, Solart was the maiden name of one of the women they hanged, Sarah Good. So I really might be descended from witches." A shiver comes over my skin as I say it out loud.

"*Accused* witches," Rachel corrects me. "The charges were trumped up. The people they hanged were all innocent. Haven't you read *The Crucible*?"

I shake my head.

"Well, you should. It's a great play. It's all about accusation and rumor." She starts telling me how Arthur Miller wrote it as a parable about the anti-Communist "witch hunts" in the 1950s, but I'm not really paying attention. I can't shake the idea that this really happened, that one of my distant relations was hanged as a witch in a town not so far from here. I get an idea.

"Hey, why don't we go to Salem after my test, for my victory lap?"

"Are you kidding?" says Rachel. "We're going to Boston, remember? We're getting dim sum in Chinatown!"

"I want to find out more about this," I insist. "You're my tutor; you're supposed to be happy when I get studious. Besides, it's *my* victory lap. Shouldn't I get to choose where we go?"

Rachel sighs. She knows me well enough to recognize my stubborn streak coming out. "You know what? Here's a deal. If you pass your driving test, you get to choose. If not, you're buying my spring rolls."

"You're on." This is such a safe bet, because I am so going to ace it.

"Most people have to retake their test at least once," Rachel says in smug tones. "I'm just saying."

Most people aren't me. I am getting my license *today*, no matter what. My whole summer depends on me having a car. As soon as I've got my license, I can start looking for jobs — there's nothing within walking distance that pays.

I can't even babysit without asking someone to drop me off and pick me up.

Must. Pass. This. Test.

The test site is in Gloucester, some twelve miles away. On the way there, Rachel gives me the lowdown. "There are two inspectors, an older man with a buzz cut and a Mexican woman with long black hair who spoke Spanish with me. You better hope you get her. The old guy is an ex-Marine, and he gave me points off for *everything*. I had him for both of my first two tries. The third time was the charm."

We're approaching the bridge near the Gloucester fisherman statue. As always, I close my eyes, holding my breath until we get across.

I don't know why I hate bridges so much, but I always have. It's that feeling of being suspended, with nothing but a thin strip of metal beneath you, then layers of air and deep water. Maybe it's because I never learned how to swim. Which is the drag of the century when you live in a harbor town with three creeks and a river, three miles from the Atlantic Ocean. For sixteen years I've been that girl stuck at the pool party praying that no one will notice she never goes into the deep end.

It isn't that I'm scared of water — I'm scared of *drowning*. I love taking showers. I even love rain. It's being *surrounded* by water that I hate. When I was little, my summer camp counselors spent hours trying to convince me that everyone floats. Not true. I'm the one who doesn't.

"What if they make me drive over the bridge?" I ask Rachel, who knows all about my phobia.

"They won't. It's a marked course in a big parking lot," Rachel reassures me. "Forget about bridges. Focus on parallel parking. That's where he got me, both times."

I take out my wallet and look at my permit, with its photo of me looking pale as a fish belly, a 45 SPF case in the land of summer tans. HAIR: BLONDE. EYES: BLUE. Which is what I put down because "it depends what I'm wearing, time of day, and the weather" isn't an option on Massachusetts state forms. My eyes change like the sky, from clear blue to blue-gray to charcoal. The one thing that's always the same is the faint rim of gold right next to the pupil. Matt once told me my eyes look like playground marbles. Nothing like having a nine-year-old brother.

We've arrived at the RMV test site, and all thoughts of bridges, witches, and my strange eyes leave my mind. Rachel parks behind the white line at the side of the road, and as we wait for the test car to finish its rounds, I twist my frizzy ponytail into a bun. That should help me look neater. I'm not taking chances.

I can't see through the glare on the windshield, but as soon as the driver — a girl about my age — opens her door, I can tell that she just got bad news. Sure enough, the passenger door's opened by a man with white hair and a clipboard.

Just my luck. I got Sergeant Harsh.

"Mmm, dim sum," Rachel says with a grin. "Looks like we're going to Chinatown."

"Don't count your chickens yet," I tell her, slamming the door shut, and I hear her shout, "Good luck!" through the window.

I bring my permit and form to the white-haired inspector, who crushes my hand in an ultra-firm handshake. I crush his right back, looking him right in his steely blue eyes. *I am passing this test today, dude. You're not going to stop me.*

I get into the driver's seat of the test car, adjusting the mirrors and fastening my seat belt. Locked and loaded.

"Pull out," says the man, and I do.

"Turning signal," he says, marking his checklist with grim satisfaction. I wince, mentally subtracting the points for forgetting to signal. I can still pass, but I can't afford to make even one other mistake.

I redouble my concentration. He takes me through all

the maneuvers — left and right turns, stop signs, passing on dotted lines, three-point turn. So far, so good.

Now it's time to do parallel parking.

There's practically no place to parallel park in our little town, but I've practiced and practiced, lining up Rachel's Volvo and Dad's well-scrubbed Honda in front of our house. This is different, though. Instead of two cars and a curb, there are lines of orange and red safety cones. If I knock one of them down, I'm a goner.

Just take it slow, I tell myself. I pull up alongside the first set of tall orange cones and back up till my front wheel's in position, pause. I crank the wheel, angling in. Then I hesitate. How far away is that row of red curb cones? I don't want to hit them. I lift my foot off the brake, backing up slowly, carefully. . . . Got it! I'm in!

The inspector looks out the window. "Too far away," he says with the same satisfied gloat in his voice. He must just adore flunking teenagers.

"Are you sure?" I beg him, though I can see my front wheel's at a bit of an angle. I notice that the second instructor, the one Rachel mentioned, is standing nearby with a clipboard, watching us. She's a full-figured woman with olive skin and she does look a lot friendlier than Sergeant Harsh.

"You want me to get out and measure?" he asks.

"Yes," I say. "Yes, please." Frowning, he opens the door and gets out, unspooling a measuring tape. Every ounce of my being is concentrated on passing this test. *Be close enough*, I think. *Don't make me lose this.*

I see him bend down with the measuring tape, and the air seems to shimmer. I think I'm about to get one of my headaches, and I have the weirdest sensation that the red cone is *moving*. Not much. Just enough.

When I look up, the other instructor is staring at me through the windshield, as if she saw it happen, too. The look in her eyes gives me chills. I'm still holding my breath as my instructor straightens up, hiking up his pants by the center belt loop. He lopes back to the door and looks in at me.

"Twelve inches," he says in gruff tones. "On the dot."

My whole body floods with adrenaline. Two thoughts barrel into my brain: *We're going to Salem!* And right underneath it: *Did I* make *that cone move?*

I'm so pumped that I don't even notice we're crossing the bridge out of Gloucester. By the time I do realize we're over water, we've practically crossed it. I take in a big gulp of air, but I don't shut my eyes.

"You see?" Rachel's voice is triumphant. "It's all in your head. When you're happy enough, you forget to be scared. Am I right?"

"You're right," I admit with a grin.

"Glad to hear it. Because there's a *really* long bridge between us and Salem. It goes all the way across Beverly Bay."

Just the thought of it makes my heart pound, but you know what? My heart's pounding anyway. I can't shake the sensation that the cone must have moved, and that — somehow — I made it happen.

Does this mean I'm losing my mind?

It's one of those perfect spring days when the sky is as blue as a postcard, and everything seems to be blooming at once. I crank down my window and breathe in the heady perfume of white lilacs and freedom. I decide to forget about the traffic cone. I just got my *license*!

We head past salt marshes and farmland, and then into Beverly, a funky old mill town that seems to be full of art students with giant portfolios and hipster glasses. Then we crest a hill, and spread out before us is Beverly Harbor. I see sailboats riding at anchor, a couple of rainbow-striped windsurfers, a fishing trawler chugging out to sea.

And a humongous arched bridge.

Rachel doesn't ask me if I'm up for it, which is a really good thing, since I'd probably bail out. But once you're strapped into your seat on the roller coaster, there's nothing to do but hold on for the ride.

I close my eyes. And something inside my head tells me to open them.

Great. Now I'm on a bridge, hearing voices. It doesn't get much more psycho than that.

The bay bridge has a long arching span, so we can't see the downward curve at all. It's as if we're just rising up into thin air. I hold my breath, keeping my eyes locked ahead. *That's not water down there*, I tell myself, not too convincingly. We're just driving up a long hill. A *very* long hill. I'm in agony, fighting a panic attack.

Rachel glances at me, but says nothing. She cranks up the music, an oldies station that both of us love. Santana's 1970s classic "Black Magic Woman" is playing, and I can't help wondering if it's in heavy rotation in Salem.

"*Got your spell on me, baby,*" Carlos Santana croons, and suddenly we're at the peak of the bridge, looking down into Salem.

The breath I've been holding explodes from my lungs like a violent sneeze. Images fly through my brain like a supercharged slide-show, much too fast to see any of them in detail. Is this my life passing before my eyes, the way people say it does when you're about to die? But the flickers I manage to catch don't seem like they're from my life at all. The clothing is dark and old-fashioned, like something I've seen in a movie. Or one of my nightmares. And why do I have a strong sense of déjà vu?

Something is thumping. It might be the drums in the song or it might be my heart, I can't tell. Am I scared, or is it something else? All I know is that even the colors look brighter. I feel tingly all over, and wider awake than I've ever been in my life.

I don't even try to tell Rachel what just happened to me. I mean, what would I say? "We got to the top of the bridge, and suddenly everything turned Technicolor, like I just arrived in the land of Oz"?

Salem does have a sort of Munchkinland quality, I see as we drive into the town. The houses are mostly brick and clapboard, in the scaled-down proportions of earlier centuries, with painted wooden shutters and window boxes overflowing with flowers. Half-circle windows perch above miniature doors, and brick sidewalks buckle around marble stoops. We drive past the village green, with its Greek-temple-styled band shell, losing our way in a thicket of one-way streets before we spot a sign for the harbor and the historic district.

"Look!" Rachel points. "That's the House of the Seven Gables! Like the book."

I remember reading the Gothic, spooky Nathaniel Hawthorne novel of the same name in my freshman English class. The house looks haunted indeed — it's the color of charcoal briquettes, with different sections attached at odd angles below the triangular gables. Just beyond it is the Derby Wharf, a long pier with a single tall ship and a lone customs house looking way out of place on a broad swath of lawn. It all seems bizarrely familiar, and not just from my research or postcards I've seen — I can picture horses clopping down these same bumpy cobblestone streets with a jangle of reins and the slow creak of wagon wheels. I can almost smell sawdust and hay.

Rachel keeps driving, past the Pickering Wharf shopping district and the New England Pirate Museum, tracing the trolley route marked in bright red on the sidewalk. We spot three different witch-themed museums sandwiched between chowder houses, psychic parlors, and gift shops with names like Bewitching Boo-tique. Even the delis have vampires and ghosts on their signs; the pet shop is called Eye of Newt. It's like a witch Disney World.

The sidewalks are crammed full of tourists and families enjoying the lovely spring weather. There's no place to park. Rachel drives slowly from street to street, craning her neck for a spot that's not taken. A teenage boy in a black T-shirt is sweeping the sidewalk in front of the Double Double Café. He stares at our car and then turns toward the curb. Right where he was looking, an SUV signals and pulls out into traffic, leaving us with a prime parking space. It's not even tight — there's a narrow alley in front — so even a girl who flunked parallel parking twice can slide into it smoothly.

Rachel and I whoop and high-five. I reach into my purse for my iPhone and check the address for the library, where they keep genealogical records.

We're on the same street.

"How's that for luck?" I say as we get out of the car.

"It's like magic," says Rachel, rolling her eyes.

"Groan. How many times do you think they've heard *that* around here?" I look at the café's purple awning, hoping to spot a street number, but there isn't one, and the boy who was sweeping has gone back up the alley and through a back door.

The smell of fresh-roasted espresso beans tickles my nostrils. "Let's go in," I say on impulse. "I want a latte."

Rachel wrinkles her nose. "Let's go to the library first and then take ourselves out for lunch. We passed plenty of other nice places to eat. That Gulu-Gulu Café place looked pretty sweet."

HOWLAND MIDDLE SCHOOL

"But I want to go *here*," I say, suddenly stubborn again. I don't know why I care so much where we get coffee, but it's as if the choice has already been made and I'm following orders. *Do it*, the voice in my head says. I open the door and walk in. I can feel Rachel's irritation at me taking over, but it doesn't matter. This is exactly where I want to be at this moment: the Double Double Café.

Its walls are mauve, covered with sepia-toned vintage photos and wreaths of dried flowers. There's a counter right next to the door where a pretty barista — tall with a black rose tattooed on one shoulder — is looking right at me with eyes like a cat's.

"May I help you?" she asks. I glance up at the menu board, lettered in lavender chalk.

"Double caramel mocha," I say, as if I come here all the time and know just what to get. It's the first thing that caught my eye, and it sounds delicious.

Rachel pores over the list of drinks, frowning at too many choices. "Green tea, rooibos, cappuccino . . ."

"Get an iced chai," I tell her. "You always do."

"You know me too well," she says with a smile, looking around for a table. There's a small round one right next to the window, with sun pouring over the lace tablecloth. We take seats across from each other and gaze out at the street.

Tourists stroll up and down, toting shopping bags from the Witch Dungeon Museum and Fangtastic Foods. A girl in a black velvet dress and Red Riding Hood cape bounces past us. A basset hound trots along next to her. A couple of reenactors in Puritan costumes walk by, talking into their cell phones.

"Salem is cute," I say, watching two children in face paint dance past, waving glittery wands. Behind them, their mother is wearing a pointed black hat with her pastel pink Polo shirt and golf shorts.

"Maybe a little too cute," sniffs Rachel.

"Your drinks?" says a low voice at her elbow. I look up and let out an actual gasp. It's the boy we saw sweeping the sidewalk, and really, "too cute" doesn't cover it. He is stunning. I'm stunned.

He's dark-browed and lanky, with butterscotch skin and a thatch of unruly dark hair that bristles like sea grass. He's also got really full lips and a couple of dimples that work overtime with that mischievous smile. But that's not what's socking me right in the gut, so hard I'm not sure I'll be able to breathe. It's his eyes. They're a clear, sparkling green, and splashed across one is a wedge of bright blue.

They're the eyes from my dream.

Chapter 3

TIME SEEMS TO HAVE FROZEN, BUT SOME-
how in this instant that's lasting forever, the boy with those
eyes must have handed me my double caramel mocha.
Because I just dropped it.

"Look out!" Rachel shrieks as the boy's hand shoots
forward, catching the cup a split second before it falls into
my lap. He sets it down on the table in front of me, the
whipped cream and caramel swirl barely trembling.

I stare. "Did you just catch a full cup of coffee in
midair?"

He shrugs. "I got lucky." Those dimples etch into his
cheeks as he looks at me, green-blue eyes twinkling.
"I'm Rem."

"R-E-M?" Rachel asks, her eyebrows twin question
marks. "As in *rapid eye movement*?"

Leave it to Rachel to sound like a science geek in front of a gorgeous boy. "Or the band?" I add quickly.

"Neither," he says. "As in Rémy. My dad's from Quebec."

"Oh, wow, you're Canadian?" God, could I sound any more like an idiot?

Rachel looks at me sidelong, but Rem shakes his head. "My mother's a native. Her people have lived here for ages."

"Mine, too!" I exclaim. "My ancestors landed in 1636."

Rem's eyes sparkle even more, if that's possible. "Yeah? Then I bet they met mine on the beach."

I can feel myself blushing bright red. When he said "native," I thought he meant *local*, not Native American. "So she's —"

"Abenaki," Rem says with evident pride. "How's that double caramel mocha?"

I haven't touched it, of course. I lift the mug quickly and steal a quick sip. It's insanely delicious, foamy and sweet with a buttery finish that makes me feel warm to the tips of my toes. "It's amazing," I tell him.

"I'm glad," he says, flashing those dimples again. "You've got . . ."

He gestures toward his own face, then reaches for mine instead. I freeze, but then he's tracing a little half moon on my cheek with the tip of his finger. The light from the window catches the blue streak in his left eye, and the world seems to glow in the same supercharged way it did on the bridge. Again, I have a tingling sensation of already knowing something that's happening for the first time. *We shall be together.* The voice echoes inside my head, and I realize that I've stopped breathing.

". . . whipped cream." Rem lifts his finger to show me the dot of white he just brushed off my face, and the surreal moment dissolves like a soap bubble. We're back to normal — not that there's anything normal about this guy Rem — but back to being a boy and a girl who don't know each other at all and don't really have an excuse to keep interacting. I wish I were one of those smooth-talking flirts — like Megan Keith, I think reluctantly — who can always come up with the right thing to say. But all I can manage to sputter is "Thanks."

"Anytime," Rem says with a waiterly nod. "Enjoy Salem."

"Well, *somebody* thinks he's all that." Rachel glances over at me as we leave the café, heading toward the library. "And it looks as if you agree." Her smugly correct usage of "as if" makes me bristle. You don't have to ace Honors English 24/7, hello.

I blush. "Well, did you *see* him?" I ask.

Rachel shrugs. "Sure, he was good-looking. But he thinks so, too."

That's not it at all, I think. Rem's not conceited. His self-assured presence isn't about what he looks like — it comes from someplace much older and deeper, as mysterious as the moon's pull on the tide. *Where am I getting this stuff from?* I wonder. *And how would I know? I met him all of five minutes ago.*

"I've got to admit, the coffee-cup trick was impressive," Rachel continues.

"It wasn't a trick," I tell her.

"Really? What was it?"

I don't have a good answer for that. What else would you call it? Luck, reflex, fate? I am *not* going to use the word *magic*, even though it's on every shop window and doormat in this crazy town.

I give Rachel a preoccupied shrug and take my iPhone out of my bag to recheck the address of the library, even though I remember it perfectly well. I don't want to give her an excuse to keep putting Rem down, when every fiber of my being is still feeling the buzz of his presence.

Or maybe it's just the caffeine. *Breathe, Abby.*

I fill up my lungs, drinking in the salt air. I don't have a crush on this Rem guy, I assure myself. I don't feel all breathless and lame-brained, the way I do when I see Travis. It's almost the opposite: I feel supercharged, filled with a humming energy I don't understand. It's like someone dialed up the volume on all of my senses.

And I'm already wondering how I can see him again.

The words from my nightmare come back unbidden: *We shall be together.* As simple as that. Not a question, a statement of fact.

Now I just have to figure out how to come back. Without Rachel.

The Salem Public Library is housed in an old redbrick mansion, with tall columns flanking the entrance. I'm definitely not the first person to come to the front desk and ask how to research my ancestors' roots; the hip-looking librarians look at each other, trading wry smiles before one of them pushes her chair back to give me the tour. There's a huge genealogical database with an in-house password, and a whole *room* dedicated to local history. It's tucked inside the reference room, with a clipper ship etched in the leaded glass over the door.

I survey the shelves full of books about Salem and witchcraft. "I think I might be here awhile," I tell Rachel.

"Fine with me," she says with a smile. "I could curl up for days in that reading room. Come and get me whenever you're ready." And just like that, I'm reminded of why we're so close. We know how to give each other space.

Valerie and I had been inseparable before she moved away. Every afternoon, every weekend, was spent together. Which was cool in its way, but we were like sisters, always fighting and making up, fighting and making up. With Rachel, there's not all that *drama* — we just get along. I smile back, feeling guilty for being annoyed with her on the way over, and grateful that we've dropped the subject of Rem.

I head into the local history room and take out my class notebook, wondering where to begin. First I log on to the in-house computer and start tracing the names that I already know, BENEVOLENCE FLETCHER on one side and ETHAN DALE on the other, hoping to find some connective threads. But however I search, I keep hitting the same gap I did with the websites last night. The dates just stop cold.

I better try out some wild hunches. Like Mom's middle name.

I type in SOLART. Dozens of links come up instantly, all including the name *Sarah Good.*

Sarah Good, accused witch. Sarah Good, mother of Dorcas Good.

Sarah Good, hanging.

A shudder runs through me. But what was her link to my mom's family? I stare into space, and a book on the shelf right in front of me catches my eye. The faded gilt letters along its cracked spine spell out *FAMILIES OF SALEM*.

I get up for a closer look. The leather-bound book has the musty, hide-and-glue smell of an old pair of riding boots. Intrigued, I take it off the shelf, and a tiny velvet-bound book tucked behind it falls into my hand.

The small booklet is worn and stained, spattered with dried candle wax. Its velvet cover is a deep, bottle-green color. It looks more like a diary than a library book, its uneven folios hand-stitched together. It must be centuries old.

Intrigued, I open it carefully to the center fold, where a worn strip of ribbon separates the yellowed pages. The text is handwritten in spidery pen and ink, the letters so faded they're hard to make out. It looks like a list of old recipes. Sounds right up my alley, but it's not going to help me one bit with my homework project. I'll come back to it later, after I've solved the mystery of Mom's Salem roots.

I sit back down with *Families of Salem*, skimming ahead till I find what I'm looking for:

Sarah Good's father, John Solart, was a well-to-do innkeeper in nearby Wenham. When he died, his estate was saddled with lawsuits, and

his daughter inherited all of his debts. Sarah Solart's first husband, an indentured servant, also died deep in debt. In desperation, she married itinerant laborer William Good, and they soon became homeless beggars, along with their young daughter, Dorcas. Sarah cracked under the strain. Hostile and possibly mentally ill, she was considered a public nuisance, and on February 29, 1692, she and two others were accused of practicing witchcraft.

February 29. The date sends a chill up my spine. My mother was born on Leap Day. When I was little, I thought it was terribly sad that her birthday came only once every four years, but she reassured me that it was a blessing: She'd never get old.

That part came too true.

I will never get used to the way something as small as a date in a book can make the constant, back-of-the-heart ache of losing her flare up like a sunspot. For a moment, I feel like I can't even breathe. Then it settles back down, and I pick up the book and keep reading.

Sarah Good was the first of the three accused witches to be questioned. Scorning the court,

she refused to confess, but townspeople lined up to testify against her, and she was found guilty despite her insistence that she was no witch. Since she was pregnant, she was not hanged at once, but thrown into prison, along with her four-year-old daughter, Dorcas, until her new baby was born. But the newborn died behind bars, and Sarah Good was hanged on July 19. Her last words to Reverend Nicholas Noyes, who condemned her to hang, were "You are a liar. I am no more a witch than you are a wizard, and if you take away my life, God will give you blood to drink." Years later, Noyes died of an internal hemorrhage, choking on his own blood.

When I read this last sentence, my hair practically stands on end.

Sarah Good's curse came true!

I stare at the book in my lap, my heart racing. So my possible ancestor wasn't just *accused* of witchcraft — she might have had actual powers. Does that mean I might have inherited them? But how, if they hanged her? I go back to reading, my hands trembling.

Little Dorcas remained in prison, alone and untended, crying piteously for her mother, for eight more months. Although she was finally released, and survived into adulthood, she never recovered from the ordeal. Eventually, like her mother before her, she went mad.

I can't bear to read any more. The idea of a motherless child locked in a prison cell breaks my heart. Of course she went crazy; who wouldn't?

But Dorcas survived, and I know in my bones that sometime in her unhappy life, she must have had a child. This would explain the long gap in my mother's family tree: the Solart connection, which leads in a straight line from Sarah to Dorcas to — skipping a few centuries — *me*.

Could the joke that some doddering great-uncle told my dad on his wedding day really be true? Is there witch's blood running through my veins? Is that why my sleep's filled with nightmares, why this peculiar town feels so familiar, why I can — maybe — move traffic cones just by wanting to?

My head feels like it's about to explode.

Or have I inherited something else from my forebears — not magic, but madness? There's a word for people who hear voices and see things, and it's *schizophrenic*.

I need some fresh air. I turn off the computer and hastily put the books back on the shelf, scurrying over to meet Rachel.

"I'm ready to go now," I say in a voice that comes out much too bright. I don't want her to notice how shaken I am.

She looks up from the novel she's three chapters into. "Already?"

I nod, holding up my list of names and dates. "I found what I needed. Let's go get some lunch." I'm talking fast. "I saw a Chinese place called the Panda Pavilion in Beverly. We could still do the dim sum thing."

"Sounds good to me," Rachel says, unfolding her legs from the armchair where she's been curled up, and following me to the door.

We walk back along the same sidewalk. Across the street from where Rachel parked her car, the trolley stripe cuts the crosswalk of a wide intersection, past a stone church with bronze sculptures surrounded by bloodred azaleas. As Rachel steps into the crosswalk, a heavy black truck zooms out from behind the church, barreling recklessly toward her.

"Look out!" I lunge forward, stepping in front of her. Every ounce of my being is caught up in one simple thought: *Stop.*

The truck grinds to a halt with a violent squeal of brakes, its grille inches away from my face. I can feel the heat rising from it.

Rachel looks at me, eyes wide. "Abby! What — you could have been killed! How did you know he . . ." She doesn't finish. Which is a good thing, because I couldn't answer.

Shaking, I hold out my hand and Rachel takes it. We finish crossing the street in silence. There's a lingering smell of scorched diesel, a hiss as the driver releases his brakes and rolls gingerly back into motion.

"Thanks," Rachel says. "That was *scary.*"

I'd have to agree.

Just as we're about to get into the Volvo, I look up and into the front window of the Double Double Café. Rem is standing stock-still at the table where he caught my coffee cup, staring at me through the glass.

Once again, I feel that surge of magnetic connection between us. It's not just adrenaline from the near-accident — it's like I can *hear* his voice right through the glass, though his mouth hasn't moved.

You're learning already. I knew you'd come back.

My heart's beating fast as I wrench my gaze away from those weird green-and-blue eyes. Learning what? How could he possibly know what was going to happen, or when I'd come back? With a pang, I recall the exact words I told myself as we were leaving.

Come back without Rachel.

My blood runs cold. I hadn't been wanting my friend to get hit by a truck! I'd only wanted to see Rem again without feeling her judgment.

I swallow hard, trying to calm down my heartbeat. *Okay, let's get real here,* I tell myself. I did *not* make anything happen. I couldn't have, even if I had that power. I *rescued* Rachel from the speeding truck; I didn't send it to get her. And neither did Rem.

All this goes through my head in a split-second jumble, like uncontrolled lightning, before I have a chance to remind myself of some important facts:

A) Magic doesn't exist.

B) Even if it does, it's got nothing to do with me.

C) I don't even *know* this guy Rem. He's just some cute local who works as a waiter. Nothing supernatural about that — just an after-school job, like the one I'll be looking for now that I've gotten my license.

Rem turns his head toward the bookshop across the alley from the Double Double Café. There's a "HELP WANTED" sign in its window. Was that there before? I'm positive I would have noticed it; I've had my eye out for jobs ever since I turned sixteen, especially now that summer is coming.

I look back at Rem, but he's busy wiping the crumbs from a table. I turn back to the bookstore. The Celtic-looking letters across the green awning read "SPIRAL VISIONS — Books, Crystals, Transformation for Spirit and Mind."

I inwardly groan at the New Agey sound of it all, but why not? The store is probably no stranger than anything else that's gone on today, and the only jobs I've seen listed in want ads are for registered nurses, auto technicians, and Zumba instructors. A bookshop sounds much more my speed.

"I'd like to step in there for a moment," I tell Rachel.

She looks up at the awning, car keys in her hand. "I thought we were going for dim sum. I'm starving. And what do you want with a crystal shop?"

I point at the help wanted sign. Rachel's eyebrows arch. "Really?" she asks.

Yes, really. Deal with it, scientist.

I head for the store. There's a tinkle of Tibetan bells as the front door swings open, admitting us into a world of soft lighting and fabric-draped tables. Mingled harp music and birdsong is playing through speakers, and there's a sweet smell of sandalwood incense.

Normally, I wouldn't be into this sort of thing, but I can't help feeling that this is a really cool store. Near the overstuffed bookshelves are racks of exotic clothing, silk scarves, and jewelry. There are Balinese masks and batik placemats and woven baskets of trinkets. There are bins filled with polished stones, each carefully labeled with its healing properties. Glass shelves display amethyst geodes and quartz crystals, alongside bronze statues of gods and goddesses from around the world, flanked by scented candles and incense. There are tarot decks, Tibetan prayer flags, and yoga mats: something for everyone.

The woman behind the counter looks up and smiles. She's a motherly redhead with silvering roots, her wide-set eyes rimmed with smudged kohl. She's dressed in comfortable layers, a vintage kimono on top of a black linen dress and red cowboy boots, with a silver pentangle at her throat and several large turquoise rings.

"Let me know how I can help you," she says.

Something comes over me — a decisive rush that feels brand-new.

"I'd like to fill out a job application," I tell her.

She looks at me for an appraising long minute, then says, "Leo?"

"Excuse me?"

"You're a fire sign," she says. "Not an Aries, though."

"Oh! Sagittarius."

This seems to be the right answer. Her smile broadens and she nods appreciatively. "Did Rem Anders send you?"

I must look completely startled, because she laughs and says, "Never mind. I'm Dyami. Write down your name, phone number, birth date, and what days you're free. I'll be in touch soon."

That's *it*? No forms to fill out, no references from past employers? How in the world did she know about Rem? A million questions flood through my mind, along with one answer: *His last name is Anders.*

"How can you work in a place where they ask for your sun sign?" says Rachel. We've ordered our food at the Panda Pavilion, and I'm pouring green tea.

"It's a job," I say, setting the teapot back onto the table. "The pay is decent, the hours are flexible. Plus it's a cool store. It's better than restocking toiletry shelves at a Walmart. It's not like our area's hopping with jobs." I don't mention the funny feeling I have — this certainty — that I need to be working in Salem. Rachel would dismiss it as silliness.

"But that woman Diana —" Rachel begins, tying her silky hair back into a ponytail.

"Dyami," I tell her.

"*Dyami*, so sorry. *Dyami* does palm readings. You don't believe in that stuff."

"So what? If I got a job in a box office, would you expect me to love every movie? Or eat every donut if I worked at Dunkin'?" I challenge.

"Point taken," says Rachel. "It just seems so . . . *silly*."

Bingo.

"Well, I need a job, and if she wants to hire me, I'm going to say yes," I reply.

"How are you going to get there?"

I hadn't thought about that part. The main point of getting a job is to save up more money to buy a used car, but I'd need the used car to get to my job. "I'll figure out something," I say with a shrug.

Rachel raises her teacup, proposing a toast. "To your victory lap," she says. "To the only teenager in Ipswich who passed her driving test on the first try."

"Come on," I say, grinning. "There must be a couple." I'm sure Travis Brown did. He's perfect in that way.

"I'm serious, Abby. I'm really impressed. When you set your mind to something, you really make it happen."

I know she means this as a compliment, but after the parking cone weirdness and the black truck, it gives me the creeps. I push my chair back from the table.

"I'll be back in a moment, all right?" I say.

Rachel nods.

The ladies' room door is behind a bamboo screen with embroidered silk hangings that wouldn't look out of place at Spiral Visions. I switch on the light.

As I'm washing my hands, I examine my face in the mirror. Under the harsh fluorescence, my skin's even paler than usual, my changeable eyes such a light, watery blue that their gold rims look really bizarre. I look like an albino giraffe.

I reach into my purse for the blusher I always carry and my fingertips touch something velvety. It's the antique green book I put back on the shelf at the Salem Library.

Or thought I did.

How did it wind up in my bag?

The rest of the day races past in a blur. I barely taste the spicy General Tso's chicken I scarf down with Rachel, and on the drive back home, I'm still thinking about that mysterious recipe book in my bag.

When I get home, I'm tempted to run right upstairs and read it. But Dad — for once — wants to talk to me and hear about how my driver's test went, so I can't pass up that rare opportunity. Matt is moaning about how hungry he is, and feeling inspired, I offer to make a celebratory dinner.

I make a spectacular seafood paella in Mom's giant skillet. I've always loved cooking, the way that what seems like a pile of random ingredients all comes together to make something delicious when you put it over a flame. Rachel calls it practical chemistry, but I think it's a lot more like practical magic. The time I feel most like myself is when I'm in the kitchen, inventing a recipe out of thin air or inhaling the mingled aromas of olive oil, garlic, and saffron.

The paella is great, but the conversation at dinner is all about Matt's soccer practice. His team's big game is tomorrow, and apparently their new goalie was messing up all morning long.

"What a loser," Matt sneers.

Dad tells him, "We all make mistakes."

"Yeah. Especially him," says my brother, tossing a mussel shell onto the pile.

I tune out their sports talk, replaying my strange day in Salem — the library, the store. And a boy named Rem Anders.

It isn't until I'm getting ready for bed that I find a private moment to take out the velvet-bound book. How *did* it get into my purse? It's a mystery, sure, but somebody else must have put it in there. Books don't move by themselves. Neither do traffic cones. Waiters don't send thoughts through window glass, and delivery trucks don't obey psychic commands. There's a good explanation for all of these things, and the word is *coincidence*.

Reassured, I pick up the book again, drawn to its moss-colored cover and fragile pages. It's like touching a piece of history. The handwritten words are so faded they seem to be written in weak tea instead of ink. The slanting script and strangely formed letters are hard to make out. But as I get used to the old-fashioned handwriting, I realize that what I thought were lists of cooking ingredients are recipes for herbal potions.

One recipe reads "For the Increase of Fortune," and on the next page there's one titled "To Induce Cramping of Stomach and Vital Organs." My eyes skim over the disgusting-sounding ingredients:

One part Powdered Orris Root
One part Sour Milk
Two Drops Tincture of Fleabane
Spoonful Dried Skunk Cabbage
Veil of a Shaggy-Stalked Toadstool

The hair on the back of my neck prickles.

I'm holding a spell book. An ancient one.

Who wrote these things down, and did they believe they would actually work?

The wind's coming up. As I sit on the edge of my bed, turning the powdery pages, a light rain starts drumming the roof and the dormers right over my head. It's a comforting sound.

I turn to a page spattered with something that looks like dried egg yolk. "To Win Another's Attention," I read through the stain.

A love potion.

And there are more. As I gaze at the various love spells, the sky seems to flicker, and I hear the low rumble of thunder somewhere in the distance.

I'm overcome with the impulse to rush down the hall into my parents' bedroom, the way I did when I was little. "The clouds are just having a party," my mother would whisper, stroking my hair. "No need to be scared." And I wasn't. I've always loved thunderstorms. I was just happy to have an excuse to be with her, snuggled against her warm nightgown.

A sudden gust of wind blows my window wide open. I can't help it; I let out a gasp, dropping the book on my lap.

This is crazy. I grew up on the North Shore; I'm not scared of storms. I tuck the spell book in the back of a dresser drawer, latch my window, and turn off the lights. Then I settle down under the covers to watch the night sky.

Lilac branches scratch at my windowpane, striping the ceiling with tossing shadows. With the next flash of lightning, I hold my breath, counting the seconds until the next crash and drumroll of thunder. Sound travels five miles a second . . . so the storm must be about twenty miles away.

The distance between me and Salem.

Chapter 4

FOR THE FIRST TIME IN WEEKS, I SLEEP
soundly and wake up without any trace of a headache,
which seems like a miracle. Realizing it's Sunday, I lie back
on my pillows, enjoying the treat of just lounging in bed for
a change. The sky is a cloudless bright blue, and the tree-
tops are bursting with shiny new leaves. It's a perfect May
morning, with birds trading songs in the lilac bushes right
under my window. All the strangeness of yesterday seems to
have vanished, and I'm left with two thoughts to savor: I'm
a licensed driver, and I've totally aced this history project.

Well, almost. I still need to add these new names to the
family-tree PowerPoint that I should wrap up today. After
I fix myself a quick breakfast, I call my grandparents in
Canton, Ohio, where Mom grew up. Maybe they can help
fill in a few missing pieces.

"Why, Abby!" Grandma bubbles. "It's so good to hear from you, dear. How is school? How's your brother?"

"Matt's fine, but he's still fast asleep. Big soccer game today."

"How did they do?" asks my grandfather, who's picked up the second extension, the one with the extra-loud speaker; he's going deaf.

"It's not until this afternoon. Four o'clock," I say, raising my voice. "Guess what I found out yesterday? One of our ancestors was hanged for witchcraft in Salem. Did you know about that?"

"Oh, honey, that's just idle rumors," Grandma says, sounding a little affronted. "Stuff and nonsense."

"No, it's true," I say, and tell her what I read about Sarah Good.

"'Good' was a common Puritan name," she insists. "There are thousands of Goods in New England. It's not the same family."

"But her father's name was John Solart. Like Mom's middle name."

"What was that?" Grandpa barks into his special extension. "Did you say Solart?"

"Oh, be quiet, Leonard, you know you can't hear on the phone."

"I can hear better than you, Margaret. Abby said 'Solart.' That was Margaret's maiden name," he explains to me. "She wanted it to live on. No idea why — they were a bunch of nuts."

Now we're getting somewhere. I feel my heartbeat speed up. "What do you know about them?" I ask.

"Nothing. Just heard they were nutty as fruitcakes."

"Do any of our Solart relatives still live near Salem?" I ask him.

"No," Grandma snaps. Is it just me, or is she uncomfortable with this topic?

"Well, there's your great-aunt Gail," Grandpa says after a short pause. "But she's in a home."

Dad gives a deep sigh when I ask him if I can borrow his car. "Now it begins," he says. "First it's 'Can I have your car?' Then it's 'Can I have my own car?'"

I do need my own car, and soon, but I'm not about to get into that now. "I'll be back in plenty of time for Matt's game," I reassure him. "And it's for my homework."

He takes the Honda's keys out of his jeans pocket and hands them over reluctantly, folding his palms around mine as he looks in my eyes. "You drive safely, all right? Take it slow."

I'm touched that he cares enough to sound worried. But is he worrying about me, or his precious car?

Both, I hope.

The Dunrovan Nursing Home is one of those buildings that's trying so hard not to look institutional that it winds up looking even worse. First of all, no real colonial building would be anywhere near this enormous. And it wouldn't have a circular driveway and garage, or a wrap-around glass-enclosed porch, or wheelchair ramps on both sides of the steps. It looks like a cross between a Holiday Inn and a hospital, which is probably just about right.

The receptionist at the front desk seems startled when I tell her I've come to visit Gail Solart. I get the idea it's been quite a while since Great-aunt Gail had any guests. "She's on the second floor," the receptionist says, weighting the words in a way I don't quite understand. She hands me a stick-on guest pass with a room number, which I attach to the front of my T-shirt. Then she points the way to the elevator, down a wide hall lined with floral wallpaper.

I can hear TV and radio sounds coming from behind residents' doors, each with a name tag and bulletin board filled with family photos, silk flowers, and other mementos.

The hallway is full of white-haired people sitting in wheelchairs or using their walkers. It makes me sad to see so many old people alone on a Sunday morning. I can sense their curiosity as I go past, and make sure to smile and make eye contact with everyone. One spunky old lady raises her cane and says, "Well, hello there, young miss!"

I ride up in the elevator with a Jamaican nurse whose magenta-manicured hand rests on top of a cart full of medicine trays. "Who are you here for, darlin'?" she asks, and when I tell her, she gets very quiet. The second-floor buzzer beeps, and I follow her out.

Right away I can see why the receptionist stressed *"second floor"* in that way. The olive-drab hall smells like Lysol; there's no music playing. The doors all stand open, and inside each room is a hospital bed. If the first floor made me feel sad, this one stirs up something darker. I can't help remembering Mom in the hospital during her last weeks, surrounded by terminal patients. My stomach turns over with dread.

The few people sitting outside in the hall are in wheelchairs, their faces blank. One bald man is slumped over so far I'm afraid he'll fall out of his motorized wheelchair. It's hard not to get the idea that everyone here is just waiting to die. A lump forms in my throat. I would hate to wind up in a place like this. Anyone would.

The name tag next to room 227 says ABIGAIL SOLART. *So Gail is short for Abigail.* I get a shivery twinge as I realize that she's my namesake — or rather, that both of us might have the same namesake. Was there some long-ago Abigail? A daughter of Dorcas? Maybe my great-aunt will know. I raise my hand to knock on the door frame. "Hello?" I say timidly.

"Come on in," says a cheerful voice, and my heart lifts.

When I step into the room, a young attendant is changing a blanket, and I realize it was her voice I just heard. The patient beneath the white sheet — Great-aunt Gail, the last of the Solarts — is as still as a corpse. Her face is sallow and misshapen, her steel-gray hair loose on the pillow. From her sunken cheeks I can see that most, if not all, of her teeth must be missing. But the spookiest thing is her vacant eyes, milky with cataracts.

"Are you a relation?" the attendant asks.

I nod. "I'm her great-niece."

"You're in luck. She's been quiet today."

Why is that lucky? I wonder. That means I can't ask her anything.

The attendant continues as she pulls a blanket up to Gail's jutting chin. "With late-stage Alzheimer's, they don't have a clue what they're saying. If she starts to scream and curse, don't be offended. It's nothing personal. Just what the mind spits back out."

I nod, looking at my great-aunt, her thin form inert on the bed. My heart is suddenly racing with nerves. What am I doing here? She's nearly a hundred years old; it's no wonder she's lost all her marbles.

"This one can be a tough customer," the nurse adds as she heads for the door. "If she starts in, just remind yourself that she doesn't know what she's saying. The call button's right here if you need it." She walks out into the hall, leaving me alone with Great-aunt Gail.

I hesitate, studying her face on the pillow. She looks so completely checked out that there doesn't seem to be much point in speaking to her. But I've come all this way, and it seems even sadder to leave without even saying hello.

"Great-aunt Gail?" I say tentatively, and step right up next to the bed. "Can you hear me?"

All at once her head swivels to face me, her clawlike hand grabbing my wrist. I'm so startled I nearly scream.

"Dorcas?" she rasps. "Is that you?"

Dorcas?

I shake my head, frightened. "I'm — I'm Abigail Silva. Your great-niece, Abby."

Her milky eyes fasten on mine. "I knew you'd be coming," she says. "I could feel the energy gathering, sparks in the wind. Fire always finds a way." Her voice sounds like a gate creaking on rusty hinges.

I'm about to ask what she means about fire and sparks, but then I remember that she has Alzheimer's, so nothing she tells me will make any sense. It's strange, though — her manner is totally lucid. *She* knows what she means. And it's certainly better than cursing and screaming.

"You need to get ready, and quickly," she rattles. "The time is coming. We need you to take up your place in the circle."

"What circle?" I can't help asking. Her voice is hypnotic, like an incantation.

"It's all been foretold. You're the one we've been —"

Her words cut off abruptly, her mouth clapping shut like a clamshell. I hear the creak of wheels over the threshold as the nurse with the bright nails and dreadlocks pushes her medication cart into the room.

"Was she talking to you?" the nurse asks me, turning to Gail with a frown. "You be nice, now, you hear? She don't need none of your nastiness."

I shake my head, my mind racing. "She wasn't cursing. Great-aunt Gail?"

Gail's face has gone totally slack. It's as if she can't hear me at all. I lean closer and try again, taking her bony hand in mine. "Great-aunt Gail, it's me, Abby. I'm still right here. What were you trying to tell me?"

There's no response. Her pale blue eyes are opaque, filmy with cataracts. But just for a split second, a jolt of static electricity crackles from her fingers to mine, and I think I hear words in my head, as I did with Rem.

You are the one.

I draw back, quickly removing my hand. Did I imagine the streak of black leaping across her left eye?

I'm freaked out to the roots of my hair by my encounter with Great-aunt Gail. What did she mean by *"You are the one"*? If she even said it. Was I really reading her thoughts in that moment, or was it my imagination?

I'm itching to look at that little green spell book in my room again. I have a feeling there must be a clue in it somewhere. Who wrote these things down, all those years ago? Could it have been Dorcas Good, or somebody else in my ancestral line?

But I can't weasel out of Matt's soccer game. It's the league semifinals, and they're playing against their arch-rivals, the notorious Orange team. I have to be a good sister and root for him.

So soon enough I find myself on the Green team

bleachers with a bunch of crazed soccer moms, still mulling over Great-aunt Gail's odd words.

Midway through the fourth quarter, I realize I'm thirsty. I've barely had anything to eat or drink all day, not since I got back from the nursing home.

I'm standing in line for my water bottle and Luna bar when I spot Travis Brown's car sailing into the parking lot. His younger brother or sister must be on the opposite team.

At least he was smart enough to come late. (I could do that if I had a car!) I watch wistfully as he helps Megan out of the cute red convertible. Draping their arms around each other, they stroll toward the soccer field.

Travis is wearing a faded gray cross-country T-shirt and scuffed jeans that fit him just right. It's really not fair that he looks this good without making an effort. Megan is resting her head on his shoulder in a way that seems calculated to say, "Hey, everyone, look what *I've* got." Her outfit — white short-shorts and a pink tank that looks spray-painted on — seems to send the same message. She says something in Travis's ear, and before I know it, they've veered toward the snack shack.

Toward me.

I'm instantly slammed with self-consciousness. Maybe I should just forget about getting food and water. I slink out of the line, jamming my wallet back into my pocket, but Travis and Megan have already seen me. He gives me his usual friendly but preoccupied smile. Megan's mouth curdles into a smirk.

"Heyyy, Abby," she drawls. "You've got a . . ." She pats her left collarbone, and I realize that I'm still wearing the nursing home guest pass. Couldn't my father or brother have told me that when I got home? But that would have meant noticing me.

I can feel myself blushing as I peel it off. "Oh, sorry," I say, though I can't for the life of me figure out why I'm apologizing to Megan. Just habit, I guess.

"Were you in line?" Travis asks me.

"Oh. No, I decided I'm not really thirsty. But thanks." I scoot out of there fast and climb back up to my seat near the top of the bleachers, feeling like a total idiot. How could I not realize I'd been wearing that stupid tag all this time? And besides, I *am* thirsty. Why did I get out of the drinks line? Travis has always been perfectly nice to me. Why do I feel like I shrink down to nothing as soon as I see him?

Not that I think I'd ever have a real shot with someone like him. But sometimes I let myself imagine — what if? What if I actually managed to work up the nerve to strike up a real conversation with Travis? We were friendly as little kids — maybe he has some fond playground memories of me, too. I wonder if he still ties a bow knot with two loops.

I watch from my perch as he and Megan take seats in the front row of the Orange team's bleachers. He's holding two sodas and hands one to her. Even this smallest gesture seems gallant. She thanks him with a kiss on the mouth.

Perfect. Now I get to sit here and watch them make out for the rest of the game.

I look back at the field. The score has been tied at two and two for well over half an hour. Matt's playing forward, and even without the big number 3 on his jersey, I'd be able to spot him by the way his dark hair bounces around his head, just like Dad's. They're both really fast runners. Dad's in coach mode — charging along the edge of the field, gesturing madly, his whistle clamped tightly between his lips. He looks like a lunatic.

The players zigzag back and forth down the field. I try to guess which of the kids on the Orange team is Travis's sibling. I bet it's that confident blonde girl who's always on top of the ball — she looks like she's from the same lucky gene pool. Travis isn't watching her much, though, since Megan keeps turning his face toward hers to kiss him. It's starting to make me a little bit nauseous.

You're dating the hot boy, okay, we all get it.

Suddenly, there's a tremendous roar all around me. Someone must have scored. I look down at the goal, where a group of green jerseys is mobbing — could it be? — my kid brother. Matt just scored the winning goal, and I missed it because I was looking at Megan Keith. Does that stink, or what?

Stricken with guilt, I stand up and yell with the rest of the soccer moms as the game's final seconds tick off. They won! The team swings Matt up onto their shoulders, yelling, "Sil-va! Sil-va!"

As I join in the chant, pumping my fist for my brother, I find myself wondering what Matt will be like when he's my age. He's athletic and confident already. Might he grow up to be someone like Travis? That's a strange thought. Imagine if a Silva was actually . . . *popular.*

Dad rushes into the crowd, raising his hand to high-five his son. I've never seen him look so proud of anyone, and it gives me a pang. Will I ever get that kind of a spotlight from him? Or from anyone else?

Not tonight, that's for sure. After the game, we are off to my uncle Paulo's tavern in Gloucester. I cast a glance back at Megan and Travis as we're leaving the field. They're standing close together, Megan's hands tucked into the back pockets of his jeans. They don't see me.

I'm so consumed with thoughts of them, not to mention lingering, haunted feelings about Great-aunt Gail, that Dad driving us over the bridge to Gloucester doesn't freak me out nearly as much as it used to. Maybe it's also because I've made the much longer crossing to Salem.

Paulo is Dad's older brother, a boisterous bear of a man who spent half his life deep-sea fishing. He then passed his charter boat on to his sons — my cousins — and took over the Anchorman Tavern, a block from the wharf. Paulo loves to eat, and he added barbecued ribs, homemade lasagna, and sausage-and-kale soup to the burgers and fries on the bar menu. His wife, Rosie, insisted on draping the scarred wooden tables with red checkered tablecloths, putting a candle on each one "to make it nice." It's a favorite hangout for fishing crews, including my cousins Mikey, Roberto, and Bruce, and the testosterone level is through the roof.

Story of my life. You might think that someone who'd grown up around so many men and boys would be more at home with guys. That she wouldn't, for instance, clam up at the mere sight of Travis. But you would be wrong. I'm an outsider in my own family.

Mikey and Roberto are at the Anchorman tonight — Bruce is crewing a swordfish boat somewhere off the Outer Banks — and they make a big fuss over Matt's winning goal. "Next stop, World Cup!" says Mikey, raising a toast. All the guys in the family join in with a baritone cheer, and Roberto claps Matt on the back.

It's at moments like this that I feel like an alien life-form. It doesn't help that they're all dark and sturdy, like Matt and Dad, and I'm tall and pale as a wax bean. When we were all little, my boy cousins called me The Brainiac, a hard name to live down at family Thanksgivings. "It's a *compliment*," Mom used to say as I wailed, but even at seven, I didn't believe her. It was code for don't-let-her-on-your-touch-football-team-ever. Add that to *can't swim*, and you have a recipe for lifetime geekhood. It's no fun to be the weird sister.

My cousin Roberto is telling Dad about the new van he's buying and what kind of options it comes with. I pick at my fried calamari, which I have to admit is delicious. All of a sudden, Dad's face lights up, and he rises to greet an auburn-haired woman who's just come in. There's something about the way he moves toward her, sliding his hand to the small of her back as he gives her a welcoming hug, that makes all my instincts go into overdrive. Who is this? Why haven't I met her before?

"I'm so glad you made it," Dad says to her.

"So am I," she replies, breathless. "We had a big conference group, and everything ran late. . . . Are these your kids?"

Dad nods. "Matt put his team into the finals today. He kicked the winning goal."

"You did?" The woman beams at Matt. "That's totally *awesome*!"

I bristle. I'm sorry, she's too old to use the word "awesome." Or to wear lipstick that shiny. I can feel an edge of dislike creeping into place, and remind myself there are worse faults than trying too hard. *Don't be so judgmental*, I tell myself, judging.

"And you must be Abby," she says, turning to me with a smile. Her teeth are so white they look painted. "Joe's told me so much about you."

He has? Somehow I doubt that.

And he's told me nothing at all about you, I think as I plaster on an attempt at a smile.

"This is Danielle," Dad says, his eyes shining. "She works at the Visitors Center." The look on his face can only mean one thing: new girlfriend. Smooth move, asking her to meet us at a family event so it won't be too awkward. I wonder if Danielle was the topic he was about to mention to me yesterday morning — but then backed down.

I look at Danielle, with her navy blue blazer, pearl earrings, and hair that looks redder than nature intended. It's easy to picture her passing out tourist brochures to convention groups. Does she have any clue she's the latest recruit in a long line of women who can't hold a candle to Mom?

"How did you meet each other?" I ask in as friendly a tone as I can.

"At the shop," says Dad.

"Joe fixed my hard drive," says Danielle, sliding onto the banquette beside him. "I get the feeling that he can fix just about *anything*." She pats Dad's hand possessively, flashing a flirtatious smile. Just like that, my dislike of her clicks into place.

Paulo comes by our table, bringing Danielle a glass of sangria and pumping her hand like he's met her before. So have my cousins, it seems. Did everyone know about this except me?

My appetite's gone. I push my calamari plate over to Matt, who's been eyeing it greedily.

"You're not gonna finish that? Cool!" he says, helping himself to a fistful and washing it down with ice water; he's already finished two root beers.

I stare at the candle in its amber jar. The music in here seems too loud. The bass thumping out of the jukebox is competing with boisterous bar conversation, and I'm getting one of my headaches. I lift my forefinger and thumb to the bridge of my nose, pinching the pressure points hard, but it doesn't help. Neither does closing my eyes.

When I open them, Danielle's shrugging out of her blazer. Her blouse is some kind of faux silk, with a ruffled neckline and billowy sleeves that remind me of a sailboat yawing in wind. As her arm sweeps across to clink glasses with Dad, I have an unbidden vision of that puffy sleeve bursting into flames.

A split second later, it does.

Danielle shrieks. Matt gapes as Dad upends his water glass, ice cubes and all, dousing the flames and then smothering them with his coach jacket, just to be sure. "Are you okay?" he breathes. "Did you get burned?"

Danielle shakes her head, lifting her charred, dripping sleeve. "You were like lightning," she marvels, staring at him.

I'm staring, too, but not at the mess on the table or even at Dad's slightly soggy new girlfriend. *Like lightning.* Her words echo inside my brain, backed by the same heart-pounding, adrenaline drumbeat I felt when that red traffic cone moved yesterday morning.

Did I make that happen?

Chapter 5

FIVE OR SIX OF MY CLASSMATES PRESENT their family trees before Ms. Baptiste calls on me. Makayla Graf turns out to have had an Austrian count in her family tree, and who knew that Kate Reeder's grandfather, Itzak Rabinowitz, got his surname Americanized by an immigration official at Ellis Island? But I think my family tree gets the prize.

I'm usually a nervous wreck when I have to stand up in front of the whole class, but this time my excitement outweighs my anxiety. My PowerPoint looks pretty cool, with differently colored Portuguese and Puritan branches coming together with my parents' marriage. I start with the seafaring Silva clan, and then skim down my mother's long roots. When I get to the part about Sarah and Dorcas Good, Ms. Baptiste sits forward.

"Now that's living history," she says to the class, standing up from her desk and joining me at the front of the room. "And it happened right here. This is exactly what I was talking about."

"Does that mean Abby's a witch?" Samson Hobby calls out. I feel my insides freeze as I think about Danielle's sleeve catching fire last night. About everything that happened over the very strange weekend.

Several kids laugh, but Ms. Baptiste doesn't.

"Suppose someone said so," she says, glancing around. "Would that make it true?"

I can feel myself getting uncomfortable, shifting from one foot to the other. This is all hitting a little too close to home.

"Of course not," says Kate. "It would just be a rumor."

"Suppose *everyone* said it, again and again," Ms. Baptiste presses. "Do you think you might start to believe all those rumors?" Kate shakes her head, but some other kids don't look so sure. "Can you think of a parallel situation?" our teacher asks.

"Yeah. Ipswich High School," says Samson, and I know what he means. When a girl like Megan Keith says something snarky about someone else — so-and-so getting a nose job, so-and-so breaking up — it's all over the school in no time.

Everyone laughs, but Kate raises her hand again. "Internet flaming. When someone posts something that's not even real, but the rumor goes viral and everybody starts thinking that it must be the truth. Kind of like what happened in Salem."

"Exactly," says Ms. Baptiste. "And when everybody starts thinking that something is true, we get what?"

"More rumors," someone says. "Bullying," says someone else.

Ms. Baptiste writes those two words on the board. "Anything else?"

Kate raises her hand again. "Blacklisting." Ms. Baptiste nods her head, pleased, but a few kids look blank.

"Kate? Definition?"

"When people won't speak to you, or let you work or live somewhere, because of the way they perceive you," she says, adjusting her black-framed glasses on her face. I've always liked Kate, because she's so matter-of-fact about being smart. But I've always felt too shy to reach out to her as a friend. "My grandfather," she goes on, "got blacklisted in the 1950s because someone said he was a Communist."

"Was he?" asks Branko.

Kate shrugs. "It didn't matter. As soon as the rumor got out, he lost his teaching job."

"And that is what's known as a witch hunt," says Ms. Baptiste, and I feel a small shiver. She circles the words *RUMOR, BULLYING, BLACKLISTING* on the whiteboard. "Fifteen months after the witch trials started in Salem, Governor Phipps pardoned all the accused and released everyone who was still in prison."

I think of Sarah Good and Dorcas, stuck in prison for all those long months, and remember how Great-aunt Gail called me Dorcas yesterday.

"Yeah, really big help if you're already dead," Samson Hobby remarks.

"Everyone who was hanged had their names cleared," Ms. Baptiste explains, "and their families received restitution. Essentially, the charges were all overturned."

"So no one was really a witch?" I blurt out. I'm almost a bit disappointed.

"Not according to Governor Phipps," Ms. Baptiste says. "But I think the real lesson of Salem is 'Don't always believe what you hear.' Not even in history class."

When the bell rings a few minutes later, Ms. Baptiste asks me to stay behind. I'm nervous I did something wrong in my presentation, but when I approach her desk, she looks excited.

"That's quite a family history, Abby," she says. "I think it bears looking into more closely. I'll give you extra credit for any more research you do at the Salem Library."

The library. With a guilty pang, I remember the spell book I stashed in the back of my dresser drawer. I have to return that — it's definitely an antique, and belongs in their local history room.

Besides, if I go back to Salem, I might get to see Rem again.

"I will," I promise my teacher.

"Good." Ms. Baptiste gazes over the tops of her glasses as if she's appraising me somehow. "I think you may find out some interesting things."

As I walk out to the school bus, passing the lot full of seniors' cars, I can't help wondering how I'm going to get back to Salem. If only I had my own car! I wish more than anything else on the planet I had enough money to buy one.

A ring tone inside my purse startles me. Who could that be? Rachel's a texter; and anyway, she's got orchestra practice.

"Hello?"

"Is this Abby?" The musical voice sounds familiar, but I can't quite place it. "It's Dyami, from Spiral Visions in Salem? I wondered if you'd like to start working on weekends."

"Yes!" I exclaim so forcefully that she laughs.

"Well, that's unambivalent, anyway. How's ten o'clock Saturday?"

"Perfect," I say. "I'll be there."

I hang up feeling breathless. So now I'll *really* have a reason to return to Salem. I can't wait to tell Rachel, even though she rolled her eyes at Spiral Visions. I'm about to send her a text when my phone rings again. I see on the caller ID that it's my cousin Roberto. Weird. Is he calling to say something about Dad's new girlfriend? Does he suspect I *wanted* her sleeve to catch fire last night?

"Hey, Abs, it's Roberto," he says when I answer. "I'm making a deal on this van, and they offered me half what my Jetta is worth on a trade-in. It's got a few dents — okay, more than a few, but the engine runs great. I thought maybe you'd want it."

I sure do! "How much were you thinking?" I do a quick calculation. I can't afford more than two thousand dollars.

"I'd probably put it on Craigslist for twenty-six hundred, but cousin price can be two thousand even. If you don't have it all in a chunk, we can work something out on installment. You interested?"

I stand outside my school, grinning. "You bet I am. That is so nice of you."

"No prob," says Roberto. "I'll bring it by later this week, so you can give it a test drive. Congrats on your license, kid. That's a big step."

I hang up in a daze. The news is amazing, for sure, but what really floors me is the timing. One minute I'm wishing that I could afford a car, and the next minute I've got one. Plus a job. It really does feel like magic.

I take out the spell book again before I go to bed. If I have to return it this Saturday, the least I can do is read through it first. Most of the spells require strange ingredients, like wolfsbane, St. John's wort, or hairs from the head of the spell's intended; one even asks for a tooth or ground-up bone.

Then I find one called "To Impel Objects to Move" that calls for herbs that I realize we must have in the spice rack or in our herb garden — calendula, rosemary, and hyssop. I'm supposed to mix those with birch root and a pinch of ground clamshell, which I can probably find in and around the house as well. *Why not give it a try?* I think with a tingle of anticipation. If I made that red cone move just by wanting it to — what might happen if I learned a spell to harness that gift?

I dart downstairs to the dark kitchen, trembling a little. There, I shake stray leaves out of spice jars and tea bags, moving quietly. Dad and Matt are both upstairs sleeping, and they'd think I was even weirder than usual if they saw me rooting around for herbs and spices for a spell. Then I take a flashlight out to the perennial herb garden Mom put in years ago. There's a white birch next to the hydrangea bush, and the clamshell is easy — our garden footpath is lined with shells Matt and I beachcombed on Cape Cod's Skaket Beach when we were little. I bring all the ingredients back to my room.

Somehow turning on my overhead light feels wrong. So I part my curtains and let the soft moonlight in. Using a mortar and pestle I swiped from the kitchen, I grind up the ingredients. Then, acting on impulse, I light a half-circle of seven candles I still have on hand from a blackout last winter. The candles seem like a nice magical touch.

Then I sit and fold my hands, my pulse racing. Now to actually try the incantation listed below the recipe in the book.

I feel more than a little bit foolish as I prepare to concentrate all my mental energy on . . . what? My laptop? What if the spell really works, and my laptop falls and breaks? I don't want to jinx it. How about the framed science fair certificate over my dresser? Maybe I can make it fall off its hook.

I gaze at its frame through the flickering flames of the candles. The seven small fires are hypnotic, casting me into a sort of a trance. Then I glance down into the spell book, and read out loud, my voice coming out stronger than I would have thought. I recite:

"Still ye may be
Quick may ye become
I command thee to move."

A gust of wind rattles the windowpane, and the candles all blow out at once. I stifle a scream. All right, that's pretty creepy, but it was the wind, not me. Right? And the science fair certificate's still on its hook. Unless . . . was I focusing more on the candle flames in the foreground when I recited those words?

I stare at the blackened, still-smoking wicks, and before my eyes, all seven of them burst back into flame!

Every hair on my head stands up as I hear a voice deep inside my head — neither Rem's not Aunt Gail's, but a rumbling, deep bass that seems to come out of the earth itself — saying, *Well done.*

I'm going crazy. I'm hearing voices and seeing things. Candles might blow *out*, but they don't blow back on. And yet there they are, burning in front of my eyes, the flames reaching higher and higher, like fiery fingernails. . . .

This is freaking me out. *Make it stop!*

And the candles go out again.

This time I really do scream. There's no rational way to explain this.

"Abby?" I hear Dad's voice call out through his bedroom door. "Are you all right?"

"Bad dream," I manage to stammer. He's heard that enough times to leave it at that. But this was no dream. I'm shaking and hugging myself. I stare at the curls of smoke rising from seven still-glowing wicks. The acrid burnt smell and melting wax are as real as that moon out my window. I turn my eyes back down to the spell book and know in my heart that I'm not going mad.

I'm a witch.

Chapter 6

ALL WEEK, I FEEL LIKE I'M SITTING ON TOP of the world's biggest secret. At school, I avoid Rachel, knowing that if we start talking, I'll want to confide in her — but she'll never believe me. I barely believe it myself. I text her that I got the job at Spiral Visions, but I don't breathe a word about the spell book, or Danielle's sleeve, or the voices I've been hearing.

I'm tempted every night to pull out that spell book and try more incantations, but I'm too terrified. I'm just living for Saturday. Somehow I'm certain that when I return to Salem, things will start to make sense again. There's got to be some reason all this is coming together now. Right?

My cousin drops off my new car on Friday night, and on Saturday morning, I drive it to Salem. When I reach the top of the humongous bridge, I'm filled with the same

Technicolor buzz I felt when I saw Salem for the first time. The sensation is something that I've never felt in my life: *I belong here.*

That sense doesn't leave me as I navigate the old cobble-stone streets, turn into the intersection in front of the church where I rescued Rachel from the oncoming truck, and sail into a parking spot that seems to be waiting for me, right in front of the Double Double Café. The only thing missing is Rem outside, sweeping the sidewalk. I peer through the front window, but he's nowhere in sight. The pretty barista is foaming some milk for a customer.

Swallowing my disappointment, I cross the alley. The door to Spiral Visions is locked, and I rap on the glass. Dyami comes out in a green embroidered caftan and silver sandals, flipping the sign on the door to OPEN as she lets me in. She looks at the flowery sundress and amber ear-rings I've chosen to wear, and nods her approval.

Dyami's idea of on-the-job training is as unique as her store.

"Be a customer," she tells me. "I want you to experience everything we have to offer, so you can internalize being a part of it."

Say what? It's a good thing that Rachel's not with me; she'd be rolling her eyes.

"So I should just . . ."

"Touch. Listen. See. Ask me questions. Once you know the store from the inside, we'll go over all the terrestrial details."

Like running the cash register, inventory, and packing mail orders, I guess. You know, actual work stuff.

It's surprisingly hard to just be a customer all morning long, especially when real customers start trickling in, and I'm longing to pitch in and help. Luckily, there's a lot on my mind as I browse through the books on the shelves, run my hands over silk scarves and kimonos, and examine the massive collection of magical objects. If a spell in a book can make candles go out and relight, is there something to all the rest of this stuff? Are the tarot decks, Norse runes, crystal pyramids, and statues of ancient deities more than just superstition and souvenirs?

Spiral Visions is well stocked with incense and herbs. As I try to memorize what is stored where, I recognize lots of ingredients from the spell book. I'll have to come back with a shopping list. I'm not planning on returning the spell book to the library anytime soon.

It seems pretty clear that the sensible, skeptical, almost-invisible Abigail Silva is not at the wheel on this side of the bridge. And I've got to say, I don't miss her. I'm enjoying this brand-new sensation that anything's possible.

I start exploring a shelf of "divination supplies" — crystal balls, wands, and amulets — when I find a small basket of pendulums. I pick one up, letting the crystal point dangle between my hands. I wonder how this is supposed to work. Do you ask a question and see how it moves, like a Ouija board? I'm about to ask Dyami when the crystal swings all by itself, so sharply it seems to point sideways. The hair on my arms stands on end, like a static electric charge, and I look where the crystal is pointing.

Rem Anders is standing outside the Double Double Café, holding a push broom. He's about to start sweeping the scatter of crabapple petals and dust when his broom seems to lift off the pavement.

Toward me.

His eyes follow, and when he sees me through the window, a smile spreads across his face.

Good morning, Abby, I hear inside my head, and a shivery thrill runs all the way through me as I realize something eerie.

I never told him my name.

I drop the pendulum back in the basket, my ears burning. This is ridiculous. He still doesn't know my name, and he hasn't *said* anything. I'm the one who imagined his voice in my head, and since, duh, I know my own name, so did my version of him. The real Rem Anders is still standing outside on the sidewalk, pushing a broom back and forth with his back to me.

Or maybe Rem has magical powers, too. I remember how he caught that coffee cup. *Anything's possible now,* I remind myself.

One thing's for certain: He did really smile at me, before he turned away to start sweeping. That by itself is enough to keep me afloat through the rest of the morning, feeling more than a little off-balance, but in a good way.

Dyami rings up a sale, handing a bag to an elderly customer. "Blessed be," she says, folding her hands and dipping her head in a little half bow. Then she turns toward me and tells me it's time for my lunch break.

Um, break from *what*? I've just been browsing for three hours.

But she says it's time, so it's time. My first thought is to go and eat at the Double Double Café, but as soon as I think about ordering lunch from Rem, I feel tongue-tied and self-conscious. Witchy powers or not, I've got a lifetime of shyness with boys to get over.

Instead, I walk a few blocks toward the wharf and around the corner, ducking into a funky local deli called Ugly Gus Chowderhouse. I push open the heavy wood door and walk straight into Rem, who's just bought a sandwich to go.

"Lunch break?" he asks with a smile.

Oh, those eyes. And those dimples.

I can't seem to find actual words, so I nod.

"Want to join me outside?" he asks.

I'm about to mumble a quick no, like my usual gawky-and-embarrassed self would, but I realize that I actually *do* want to join him, a lot. And he's already done all the work. All I have to do is say, "Sure." It rolls right off my tongue, as if it's every day I make lunch dates with gorgeous boys who have hypnotic green-and-blue eyes.

Rem turns to the heavyset man behind the counter. "Hey, Gus, you make Abby a wicked good sandwich, you hear?" I can feel my heart pounding all over again.

So he does know my name.

Rem brings me down to a small, grassy park overlooking the harbor. "I never eat inside at this time of year," he says, settling down near the base of an oak tree. "Salem is full of cool places for picnics."

"Did you grow up right here in town?" I ask, trying to find a comfortable perch on one of the tree's exposed roots.

"Born and bred," he says, watching me unwrap my ham and Swiss. The ciabatta roll is stuffed so full of meat, cheese, tomato, sliced onion, and shredded lettuce that I can't imagine how I'm going to get my mouth around it without squirting mustard all over my dress.

Rem flashes a knowing smile. "There is no polite way to bite into a Guswich," he says, peeling the foil wrapper back from his chicken parm grinder. "You just have to go for it."

He takes a big bite, angling in from one side and coming away with a long string of red sauce and cheese between his teeth and the roll. I can't quite make out what he says with his mouth full, but I think it's "You see?"

I do see. Smiling, I take an undainty bite of my own dripping sandwich. It's actually kind of a perfect ice-breaker. It's hard to be too self-conscious around someone when you've shared a deeply messy lunch and the laughs that go with it.

"Final score: mustard: three, marinara sauce: five," he announces as we crumple up our sandwich wrappers.

I point to his ear. "Make that six."

"No way. On my *ear*? Oh, man, that's undignified." He swipes at the spot with a napkin. "Did I get it?"

"Most of it," I tell him, laughing. He's even cuter when he seems embarrassed.

He pats at his ear. "But the sandwich was worth the mess, am I right?"

He is right. "Delicious," I tell him. We talk about favorite foods — his is watermelon — and I confess to him how much I love making up recipes. He seems impressed by that, and I blush. We compare what's on our iPods, discuss our kid brothers (Rem has two), our jobs, and anything else that comes into our heads. When I'm not looking into Rem's eyes, I feel something that I've never felt around any guy — certainly not around Travis. I feel at home, like it's okay to just be myself.

When I am looking into his eyes, it's a different story. I feel as if some hidden spark deep inside me is starting to glow like an ember, and I'm no longer sure who "myself" really is. Someone who can cast spells, who might be able to make things move just by thinking about them, and someone — the most magical feeling of all — who can share a connection with a guy like Rem and not shy away from it.

I come back from lunch feeling dazed, in a spin of happiness and total confusion. What I feel for Rem feels completely different from a crush. My crush on Travis is a breathless, fluttery, don't-get-too-close-or-I'll-faint kind of thing; with Rem, it's more *how do I already know you so well?*

I wonder if psychic Dyami is picking up on how confused and giddy I am right now. But she's reading a customer's palm at the small table next to the register, so I busy myself rehanging a group of dream catchers that someone's picked over and left on the counter.

"Do you work here?" a bearded man asks me.

I hesitate, but just for a split second. "Yes," I tell him. "What can I help you with?"

"Do you sell dragon's blood?" That isn't an herbal name you can forget. I know exactly where it is.

"It's next to the frankincense," I tell the customer. "Right over there."

He goes over and picks up three packets, bringing them back to the counter. My bubble of competence bursts as I realize I'll need to ask for Dyami's help. But she's already rising to join me at the cash register. I watch as she rings up the purchase and slips the herbs into a bag with the receipt and a warm "Blessed be."

The dragon's blood guy heads for the door, and the palmistry customer gets up to pay for her reading. "That was so helpful," she says to Dyami. "I feel like the sun just came out in my soul."

That makes two of us.

After the customer leaves, there's a bit of a lull. It seems like an ideal time to teach me the practical stuff, like using the cash register, but Dyami sends me to the bins full of crystals and polished stones, "to get to know them."

Okay. If you say so.

I pore over the cards on each bin, trying to memorize which stone is supposed to have what healing properties, but it all seems preposterous. Why would a garnet boost energy, or a malachite attract money?

Dyami comes up behind me. "Don't read about them," she says. "Use your heart knowledge. You don't even need your eyes. Let your hands guide you. The ones whose vibrations you feel have the magic you need." She passes me a maroon velvet pouch and instructs me to pick out "whatever stones call to you."

I don't know whether it's looks, feel, or instinct, but certain stones do seem to stick to my fingers. I choose about seven, dropping each one into my bag.

"Spread them out on my silk," she says, and I do. She touches her pentacle necklace, then hovers her hand an inch or two over the group of stones. "Interesting," she says, turning back to me with a satisfied smile. "All of your chakras are open. You're ready."

Ready for *what*? I wonder, but she answers before I can ask. "I'm doing a tarot reading at two. You'll take over the cash register."

"But I don't know how —"

"Yes, you do," she says briskly. And somehow she's right. Just from watching her ring up the morning's few customers, I seem to have learned all the register codes. Or maybe it's part and parcel of discovering that I'm a witch: Things that used to be hard for me aren't anymore. Is this how it feels to be confident?

The rest of the afternoon flies by, and as we're getting ready to close up, I notice the velvet pouch and head over to put the stones back in the bins.

"What are you doing?" Dyami says. "Those are for you."

"Really?"

She reaches for my right hand, turns it over, and studies my palm. Something she sees makes her eyebrows go up, but she doesn't explain what it is. She just places the small maroon pouch on my palm and folds my fingers over it. "It's good energy. Keep it close by. You'll be needing it soon."

A week ago I would have asked what she meant by that, but I don't. Whatever it is, I believe her.

On Monday morning, I lay out the energy stones in a line at the base of my bedroom mirror. Their different shades make a rainbow of sorts, and the one in the middle, a vivid green malachite/azurite mix, reminds me a lot of Rem's eyes. I remember the splatter of sauce on his earlobe and can't stop from smiling as I work my brush through the unruly thatch of my straw-colored hair.

I've always been ashamed of my frizzy bed-head, and have spent countless hours trying to flatten it down with hot irons and all kinds of mousses. Invariably, I would give up and just pull it into a tight ponytail, hoping the back wouldn't bush out too badly.

I'm reaching for one of my giant collection of hair ties and clips when I catch a look at myself in the mirror. The sun's pouring in through the window and in its warm light, my wild tumble of frizzy curls looks almost . . . pretty.

Why not leave it loose for once? Who says that I can't change my look if I feel like it?

I walk down the staircase and into the kitchen feeling self-conscious. But Dad barely glances away from his morning paper, and Matt's playing some kind of video game between bites of cereal.

Hey, guys, good morning to you, too, I think as I pour myself grapefruit juice. If I set my hair on fire, maybe they'd notice it.

I'm driving my new car to school, so I don't have to deal with the kids on the bus. I park next to Rachel's navy blue Volvo, and am happy to see she's still wrestling her cello case out of the back. I've missed talking to her.

I feel a little guilty — ever since that first weekend in Salem, I haven't been spending as much time with her. I know Rachel's a skeptic, and if I tried to tell her about Dyami's energy stones — not to mention what happened the night I recited the spell — she'd look at me like I was out of my mind.

As soon as she straightens up, she notices that my hair's loose.

"Hey, it looks great that way," she says with a warm smile. "I wish my own hair had some shape to it."

Funny, I've always envied her silky black hair. I guess whatever you don't have yourself is what you think looks best.

Slinging her arm over Igor's black case, Rachel asks me if I'm planning to come to the Honor Society meeting today after school. "We're organizing that bake sale for next week," she reminds me. "I'm hoping you'll make some of your killer cupcakes. Or those mocha-cream tarts you made last time I came over for dinner, or your caramel brownies. Anything you feel like baking."

"Of course," I say. This is one topic that we can agree on.

Together, we walk through the school entrance doors. I touch a quick hand to my hair, still not used to feeling it loose. Rachel and I part ways and I head for history class.

Samson Hobby's the first person to comment on my change of look. "Letting your freak flag fly, Abby?" he snarks. "Be afraid. Be very afraid." His Goth friends all snicker, but one of the girls in the group gives me a sideways approving glance, as if I've turned secretly cool.

But the most satisfying reaction is Travis Brown's. When I turn the hall corner, running into him and Megan, his head swivels around like a comedian's double take. It's as if he's never seen me before in his life.

Well, maybe he hasn't. I was a real pro at being invisible, back in the day.

"Hi, Abby," he says with a goofy smile that makes my heart melt. "You look terrific." My cheeks flame. Did he really *say* that?

"Thanks," I say, fighting the urge to add, *You, too.* But I can't fight the smile he's brought to my face.

Megan tugs hard on his hand, looking very annoyed, which makes the moment feel even sweeter. I bounce past them and continue down the hall with a satisfied smirk. Life isn't so bad, I think. I could get used to this kind of attention.

Never get smug. That's the lesson, I guess. I'm enjoying my first day of visibility at Ipswich High School when I make a fatal mistake. During lunch, I go to the cafeteria monitor and get a hall pass for the girls' room.

When I come out of the stall, they're waiting for me. Megan and her henchwomen, Amber and Sloane.

Before I can react, Amber and Sloane approach me and stand so close that I can feel their breath. I'm basically cornered into the wall. I'm so freaked out by the suddenness of it that I can't even move or push past them.

When Megan walks slowly up to me, setting her face a few inches from mine, I cringe and shrink back from her, terrified. You don't lose years of reflex with one change of hairstyle.

"What makes you think you can flirt with my boyfriend?" Megan demands.

"I didn't," I say. Which is totally true. Travis said hi to *me*. He complimented *me*. I just said thank you.

Sloane reaches out and gives my arm a quick, vicious twist. "Shut up, loser." The pain is as surprising as her touch — I've always known these girls could be cruel, but didn't think they'd be capable of violence. I feel afraid in a new way.

"Freak!" Amber chimes in.

Megan's manicured hand twines into the roots of my hair, twisting tighter with every phrase. "You don't flirt with Travis, you don't talk to Travis, you don't *look* at Travis. He's not into you. He's not ever going to be into you. Got that?"

I nod. Megan lets go of me, tossing her lustrous dark hair as if she's the star of her own private shampoo commercial.

"Come on," she says to her goon squad. "She is totally not worth our time."

"Totes," echoes Amber in her squeaky voice.

Sloane hisses, "Loser times ten." Her sharp brown eyes glitter with hatred, as if she's reluctant to leave me alone.

The three of them head for the bathroom door, and I feel a wave of relief. But then Megan turns back to look at me. "I just figured out who she looks like with her hair down."

"Who?" says Amber eagerly, poised to crack up at whatever she says.

Megan pauses. "Big Bird."

All three of them burst out laughing, and Amber says, "That's *perfect*!" She shrieks with hysterical laughter as if Megan's the star of her favorite sitcom. "Big Bird! Oh, you are *so funny*!"

As the door shuts behind them, I finally exhale. I've never been bullied like that before — nobody bothered to pick on me. This is the dark flip side to being visible.

I can feel my scalp burning and my eyes sting with tears. But more than that, I can feel heat in my veins, fueled by humiliation and tamped-down rage.

I could make something bad happen to you, I think. *To all of you*. I imagine Megan's hair falling out, Sloane's hands turning into claws, Amber losing her voice forever.

Then I stop myself and shudder. What if the things I'm imagining actually happened, the way Danielle's sleeve caught on fire?

Even if I have magical powers, do I want to waste them on someone like Megan Keith? Or her cruel sidekicks?

You know what? I just might.

I look at myself in the bathroom mirror. My hair's even bushier now, like a clump of blonde Easter grass, but that's not what grabs my attention. I lean in closer to look at my eyes. They're a stormy gray-blue today, so the gold rims stand out more than usual. So does a yellowish, lightning-bolt streak near my left pupil that I've never noticed before. It looks really witchy.

I flash back to the velvet-wrapped spell book in my bedroom. I remember the yolk-splattered page I was reading when that thunderstorm started. I can vividly picture the spidery handwriting in my mind's eye:

To Win Another's Attention

The love potion. Would that work on Travis? It would be such sweet revenge to get him to start paying attention to me. Not to mention my own dream come true. And if Megan breaks up with him over it, so much the better. He doesn't deserve a mean girlfriend, no matter how perfect her figure and glossy her hair. He'd be much better off with someone who's been head over heels for him ever since he was tying her shoes.

Someone exactly like me.

Late that night, when I'm alone in my bedroom, I take the spell book out of my dresser and start flipping through it. Some of the spells for revenge are so nasty they make my blood run cold. No matter how horrible Megan and her friends might be, I would not want their fingers to actually blacken and rot and their nails to fall off. But winning Travis's attention? Now, that would be heaven.

I close my eyes, concentrating, and open the book to a random page. *If it's the right spell, then I'll try it*, I think. I open my eyes, and it is.

I don't even care how crazy this sounds anymore. My definition of sane has become very flexible.

I skim down the list of ingredients. I don't have all the tinctures and herbs it requires, but the ones that I'm missing will be easy to pick up at Spiral Visions. Where I'm going to be in exactly five days.

Chapter 7

I GO TO WORK EARLY ON SATURDAY MORN-ing with a list of ingredients tucked in my pocket. But Spiral Visions starts busy and stays busy all morning. The summer tourist season is gearing up, and I can see why Dyami wanted some help on the weekends.

Right before lunch, there's a bit of a lull. Dyami is reading a customer's palm, and there's nobody else in the store. Could this be the moment to pick out my potion ingredients? I head to the bins by the window to look through the herbs. The church clock strikes noon, and I look outside and see something that makes my jaw drop.

Megan Keith is crossing the street, closely followed by Amber and Sloane. *No.* They're heading right for Spiral Visions. But maybe they're just walking in this direction, and then will turn and enter a different store?

No such luck. Any doubts I might have disappear when Amber checks an address on her iPhone and points to the awning, as all three dissolve into giggles.

Oh, where is a speeding black truck when you need one?

They step onto the sidewalk and come in through the open front door, parting the shimmering curtain of moon and star beads we just hung in the doorway.

"What an *adorable* shop!" exclaims Megan in arch, artificial tones. "Look, they sell *incense*!"

"Ooooh," Amber and Sloane say in unison, making it clear they've rehearsed this.

"And ritual objects. I need me some new ritual objects. My old ones are just such a drag." As usual, Amber and Sloane think she's hilarious and crack up on cue.

"May I help you with something?" I say in my friendliest, most professional voice. I refuse to act scared, like I did back in the girls' room at school. That might be their turf, but Salem is mine.

I remember a quotation from Eleanor Roosevelt that Mom once said to me: "No one can make you feel inferior without your consent." These wise words ring in my ears as I face the three girls. Megan can do what she likes; I'm not going to give her my consent.

"If it isn't Big Bird. Do you work here?" says Megan. Her tone makes it perfectly clear that she knows that already, but can't resist taking a poke at me. How did she find out that I had this job? Did she overhear me telling Rachel about Spiral Visions at school?

Dyami looks up from her palm reading. She's wearing a rust-colored crushed velvet jacket, with a tie-dyed purple scarf knotted over her hennaed curls. With her usual kohl-ringed eyes and oversized earrings, she looks like a cross between Janis Joplin and Captain Jack Sparrow.

"Could you please keep your voices down?" she asks politely. "I'm giving a reading."

"Oh, wow, I don't mean to, like, ruin the vibe," says Megan. I could slap her for being so rude and sarcastic. *Keep your temper*, I remind myself as she turns from Dyami toward me.

"Your website says that you sell crystal jewelry for all occasions. Is that correct?"

I nod, thin-lipped. Where is Megan heading with this?

"How about something to wear to the prom?" she asks. *"With my boyfriend."*

The same boyfriend I'm about to cast a love spell on, I think, and I try to fight back the smile that steals over my face. Megan looks confused at the change in my expression, but I quickly rearrange my features so that they're neutral once more.

"The jewelry is right over here," I say evenly, leading her over to the glass case at the counter.

"Oh, sweet," she says, making a big show of looking at all of the necklaces. "Wolves and yin-yang signs. My favorite!"

"The peace signs are groovy, too," Amber says sarcastically.

"I'm digging the hex rings," says Sloane.

"I'm thinking crystal," says Megan. "What do you say, girls? The cut-crystal heart or the Herkimer diamonds? I think the heart."

"Totally," Sloane says, as Amber says, "Absolutely."

"May I try it on?" Megan says. I nod curtly and hand her the heart-shaped pendant she's pointing at, which hangs from a long silver chain.

She twists her glossy brown hair into a loose knot on top of her head. "I'll be wearing it up, of course." With a satisfied smile, she fastens the clasp at the back of her neck and checks herself out in the mirror, turning from side to side to admire her reflection.

"What do you think?" she asks. "Would Travis like this?"

"Of course he would. You look totally *hot*," says Amber.

"Slamming," Sloane echoes.

"What about you, Abby? Do you think it's a good choice for prom night?" Megan demands. Amber and Sloane are both looking at me.

"It's a very nice crystal" is all I will say.

"I'm so glad we agree. It'll look really great with my prom gown," Megan says with a smirk, digging into her wallet. "I'll take it."

I turn over the box it was in. "It's a hundred and twenty-nine dollars. The chain is real silver."

Megan doesn't blink as she hands me her platinum MasterCard. "Nothing's too good for my Travis," she purrs.

Even Eleanor Roosevelt would feel like choking her. As I run Megan's card through the imprint machine, I remind myself about the spell. The love potion. If that works as well as the candles, she's going to be sorry.

Dyami finishes her palm reading just as Megan finally sweeps out of the store with her giggling friends. Dyami comes to stand next to me, watching them go.

"Very young souls. Little jabbering monkeys." She shakes her head with a jangle of earrings. "What that girl doesn't know is that high school is the absolute peak of her life. She may be on top now, but the rest is a long, slow downhill. And the people she picks on are just getting started."

Dyami turns toward me. Her eyes have the trancey expression she gets when she's giving someone a reading. "But who is this — is his name Trevor?"

The tips of my ears get warm. "Travis."

"He likes you a lot," says Dyami, a smile spreading over her face. "It's no wonder the queen of the monkeys feels threatened."

The queen of the monkeys. Now there is a phrase to bring joy to my heart. And if she thinks Travis likes me now, wait till I get him under my spell.

As I head out for my lunch break, my mind's turning over and over. Could Dyami really be right about Travis? Her instincts are usually correct, but he's never been more than generically friendly or looked at me twice till this week. Plus he's dating the queen of the monkeys.

I'm trying to figure it out when I run into Rem, coming out of the pizza place I'm going into. My heart lifts as soon as I see him. I've noticed that he has an uncanny instinct for turning up right where I'm heading. It's as if he has some kind of internal timer, taking his lunch breaks or going out on an errand exactly when I do. He always seems happy to see me, and always acts like it's a total coincidence, which, who knows, it might be. Sometimes people just have a weird synchronicity, and you run into them *everywhere* for no reason at all. I don't understand it, but I'm not complaining.

He holds up a pizza box. "How do you feel about pineapple?"

"Great in a fruit salad. Lousy on pizza."

Rem grins. "Perfect. I got slices with everything but. And there's plenty for two."

"Really?" I say. "Can I pick up some sodas?"

"Sure," he says. "There's a deli right next to the park I'm thinking of."

It's obvious Rem knows all the non-touristy local places to find a cheap lunch, away from the trolley route and the pedestrian shopping mall. I get the sense that there's a second Salem behind all the quaintness and witch kitsch, where the people who live here go to get haircuts, do laundry, and buy discount shoes. And there must be a high school, right?

I ask him that as we settle onto a bench with our pizza and drinks.

Rem nods and points toward a tall smokestack on the horizon. "It's over that way, by the power plant and the boatyards."

"Is that where you go?" I ask, opening my can of soda.

He shakes his head. "Graduated last year. I've been doing the gap year thing, earning some money for college."

"Do you know where you're going?" I ask him.

Rem hesitates. "I know where I'd like to go, but I'd rather put money aside for it first than take on lots of student loan debt. You know how it goes."

I do indeed. "So you're working full-time right now?" I ask as he hands me a pizza slice piled high with so many toppings I can't see the sauce.

"Part-time at the café, but yeah. I've got a few other odd jobs. House-painting, boat-painting, stuff like that. What about you? Are you starting to think about college?"

I nod, waving my hand to indicate that my mouth is full. Rem flashes a grin as he watches me speed up my chewing.

"No, let me guess," he says. "Science, right? Chemistry, botany . . . chef school?"

My eyes open wide. "How did you know? Did I tell you that?" It's been my secret ambition to train as a chef, but since I'm good at science and my mom was a botanist, everyone's always assumed I would follow her footsteps.

"How did you know?" I ask Rem again. This time *his* mouth's full of pizza.

After he swallows, he shrugs and says, "I just picture you with a mixing bowl. Grinding up herbs in a mortar and pestle."

Um, that actually might be the potion I'm planning, but I'm not about to tell Rem about *that*. He'd probably think I was out of my mind. And I'm certainly not going to tell him anything about Travis.

Not for the first time, I wonder if Rem's got a girlfriend. It's hard to believe that someone as gorgeous as he is doesn't have someone in love with him.

Sometimes I wonder if that someone might even be me. But I'm not going to tell him that either. The list of things I'm not telling is growing by leaps and bounds. But it's all so confusing. I look at Travis and see someone I've adored my whole life. I look at Rem and see . . . what? Someone I barely know, but can't take my eyes off whenever I'm with him. Someone who seems to understand me instinctively.

After we finish our pizza, Rem leans back onto his elbows and squints at the sky. "We better head back," he says. "Going to start raining soon."

I look up at the sky. It's clouded over since we started eating, but it doesn't look at all threatening. "How can you tell?"

He shrugs. "I can smell it. The ozone." He folds up the pizza box, dropping it into a nearby trash can. Like every trash can in Salem, it features a graphic of two legs in striped socks and pointy black shoes, next to a twig broom. You can't escape witches around here.

I swallow my last few sips of soda, reluctant to leave, but Rem's right: By the time we walk back to the Double Double Café, the sky has turned gunmetal gray.

The first few drops spatter the awning as I stand next to Rem, hoping he'll hug me good-bye. Not a boyfriend-y, full body embrace, just that little brush-touch most friends do when they're saying good-bye to each other. But I've noticed that Rem's not a toucher. In fact, he has both hands jammed into the back pockets of his jeans, which does very nice things for his biceps, but also seems like a statement, a small way of keeping his distance.

"Well, bye," I say, letting the moment stretch awkwardly. Maybe if I just stand here doing nothing, he'll figure it out. I notice the cat-eyed barista at the Double Double Café watching us through the window. I wonder if she has a crush on Rem Anders. It wouldn't surprise me.

"You better get into the store. It's about to start pouring," Rem says. I nod and take off, feeling a slight sting of disappointment as I cross the alley. It isn't as if I expect this hunk to be swept off his feet by my pale, gawky self. It would make perfect sense if he just ignored me, but why does he have to blow so hot and cold? One minute he's seeking me out, almost seems to be flirting with me, and the next he's completely indifferent. I can't get a read on him, which means that I never know how to behave. I don't understand how I can feel so connected to him and so unsure of him at the same time, but Rem's nothing if not full of mysteries.

All afternoon the rain comes down in sheets, and the only customers who come in are two surly tourists who scuttle inside to get out of the rain for a couple of minutes. I try to entice them to browse, but they don't even bother to answer me. They stand side by side right in front of the door, frowning at the rain as if it's out to get them, and blaming each other for everything. "If you hadn't spent so much time in the store . . . If you ever remembered to bring the umbrella . . ."

"It'll let up soon," I say, doing my best to sound like a friendly employee, but fervently wishing they'd both go away.

Just at that moment, the rain stops.

"Thank god," says the woman, whose husband is already pulling her out the door, as if he can't wait to get out of this horrible store. As they cross the street to their minivan, a fresh gust of wind-driven rain soaks them both to the skin. I can't help feeling satisfied. Serves them both right for being so rude.

The lights in the store flicker and then cut out. So does the music.

When I turn away from the window, Dyami is looking at me with a strange expression.

"Is it a blackout?" I ask her.

She nods. "It certainly is." She quickly lights some candles, then reaches over to pick up her tarot deck. "Let's take a look at your cards, shall we? I'm sensing we'll have the place to ourselves for a while."

Probably true. It's already pouring again.

Dyami spreads out her silk, and lays out four objects in each of its corners: a conch shell, a small piece of driftwood, an old Chinese coin, and another candle.

"The four suits of the tarot deck represent the four elements," she explains. "Earth, water, air . . ." She strikes a match, lighting the candle. "And fire."

A tingle runs right up my spine. It's partly the shadowy light and the echoing sound of the rain on the roof, but the mood in the store is suddenly deeply mysterious. The light from the candle seems way too bright, as if that single flame holds a bonfire within. I can't keep my eyes off it.

Dyami takes out her card deck and places the whole stack between my palms, wrapping her own hands around mine. She shuts her eyes, taking a few long, deep breaths. Then she opens her eyes again.

"Cut the cards," she instructs. "Once, twice, three times to the left."

I obey. She picks up the reshuffled deck and starts dealing out cards in a cross pattern, turning them faceup one at a time. I'm not prepared for the raw strength of the painted images. A man hangs upside down by one foot . . . a heart is pierced by three swords . . . a body lies on the ground, pierced by a row of ten more swords . . . two figures are thrown from a stone tower struck by a lightning bolt.

Dyami's brows knit together. She deals out another card with a high priestess seated between black and white columns, the crescent moon at her feet.

"So much power," she murmurs.

What does that mean? Is it good or bad? I could do with some hints around now.

Dyami turns over the next card, and her face relaxes into a smile. "Well, I know who *this* is." She points at the image: a young page by the edge of the sea, holding a goblet with a small fish peering out at him.

Behind me, I hear the front door swing open. Is it the wind?

"And there he is now," says Dyami.

I turn to see Rem, his hair spiky and wet from the rain. My heart jumps at the sight of him.

"Have you got some candles?" he asks. "The café's all out."

"What kind do you want? We're candle central," Dyami says, heading into the darkened stockroom.

Rem crosses the room to the table where I'm still sitting. He looks down at the tarot spread, and I see his jaw clench.

"What are you doing this for?" he says with an edge in his voice.

"Just for fun," I tell him. "No customers, no electricity, so we decided to . . ."

"Fun?" Rem's voice sounds angry, contemptuous. "Don't mess around with the elements. Ever."

"What are you talking about?" I demand, bristling at his tone.

"This isn't a game. Not for people like us."

What?

Before I can ask him what he means by that, Dyami comes out with a carton of votives. "Here you go. These ought to hold you."

"Thanks," says Rem, taking the candles from her. His grin parts the clouds on his face as if nothing had happened. "Bye, Abby," he twinkles, his dimples on full display. What is *with* this guy?

Just as he reaches the door, Rem turns and looks back

at me, and I have that same strange sensation of hearing his thoughts.

Don't play games. This is real, says the voice in my head, backed by a surge of electrical hum as the lights blink back on.

Rem's warning reverberates inside my head as I circle the store, picking out all the powders and herbs that I need for my love potion for Travis.

I hear it again in my room late that night, as I line them up next to the spell book, a mixing bowl, and yes, a mortar and pestle. But I don't want to listen. I think of the way Megan and her friends cornered me in the bathroom at school. I hear their mocking laughter when they tracked me down at my job — just because Travis was nice to me! — I think of sweet, generous Travis, and my anger rises all over again.

She doesn't deserve him. I do. It's that simple.

I take a deep breath. The night air feels electric and newly washed in the wake of the rainstorm. I can smell the familiar salt nip of the ocean a few miles away, mingled in with the heady flower perfumes of late spring.

Dad is back from his latest dinner date with Danielle, and I can hear his steady not-quite-a-snore down the hall.

Matt is out like a light in his room, too. The house is all mine.

I pick up the spell book and open it up to a random page. It's the spell I was looking for. My breath catches with the reminder that I really do possess magical powers.

Like any good cook, I start by assembling all the ingredients I've collected. This spell really is like preparing a recipe, because after I've mixed up the potion, I need to get Travis to swallow a spoonful. Sounds kind of tricky, but I've got a plan.

I reread the first line of the spell:

Obtain an Image of the Beloved

I open my desk drawer and take out a photo of Travis I cut from the newspaper sports page. Even in the grainy newsprint likeness, his wide grin melts my heart. As the recipe instructs, I place the photo on a plate, and add a photo of me — a random snapshot Valerie took of me on the front steps of my house — facedown on top of it. The next step of the spell calls for crumbling dried rose and marigold petals together and sprinkling them in a circle around the photos.

Then I make use of my haul from the store today. I mix two drops of lavender oil, one of wildflower honey, and three threads of ginseng root into a sticky paste, which I dab on the photos' four corners. I grind pinches of witch hazel, thyme, periwinkle, and white sage in the mortar and sprinkle the fine powder over the photos as well.

Now it's time to burn them. I've set up the same semicircle of seven white candles as I did during the last spell. Lighting them one at a time, I recite:

> *"Forsaking all others*
> *Turn thine eyes to me*
> *So mote it be*
> *It is done."*

The flames of the candles flare up and back down. Following the spell's instructions, I pick up the candle in the center and use it to set fire to the photographs, concentrating all my thoughts on Travis as they burn. I gather the powdery, herb-scented ash in a silver spoon, tipping it into the velvet pouch.

There. That part is done. Now I just have to get Travis to swallow it.

I'm going to be doing some baking tomorrow.

Chapter 8

I SPEND THE NEXT AFTERNOON IN THE kitchen, turning out batches of chocolate-chip cookies, gingersnaps, caramel brownies, and lemon-coconut cupcakes. Mixing the batters and lifting the fragrant baking sheets out of the oven fills me with a heady joy. This is really what I'm meant to do. As I sample a bite of a brownie — still warm, so the caramel swirl gushes onto my tongue — I find myself thinking not of Travis, but Rem. I think of the marinara sauce splashed on his ear and the pizza-with-everything lunch when he guessed I was dreaming of chef school. *I'll have to bake him something special someday*, I think with a smile.

Matt's soccer friends Kevin, Ridley, and Griffin are all hanging out at our house, and they make such excited, frequent raids on the cooling racks that I'm afraid I won't have anything left to sell at the National Honor Society bake sale, much less to sprinkle with hex powder for that special someone. One of those cupcakes has Travis Brown's name on it.

The bake sale is after school on Tuesday, right outside the gym. There's a track meet today, and we're trying to catch hungry spectators, plus any athletes who might need a last-minute carbo-load. I'm sitting with Rachel and Kate Reeder, my stomach aflutter with nervous excitement. I can't quite believe that I'm going to go through with this. Plus there's the added anxiety that the special cupcake with hex powder under its coconut icing might some-how find its way to the wrong jock. I've set it aside in an otherwise-empty tin, just to be on the safe side, but you never know.

Most of the track team has already jogged past our table, some of them stopping to pick up a treat on their way to the track. When Travis comes out of the gym, look-ing handsome in his maroon singlet and track shorts, my heart starts to race. I concentrate all my energy on making him turn toward our table. He does. It's like playing a video game with a joystick. *Okay, Travis. Now you look right at me.*

He does that, too, and I hand him the cupcake I made just for him. "Home-baked," I tell him. "My treat."

Travis grins. "Hey, thanks," he says, taking a giant bite. My breath catches as he swallows.

So mote it be.

Travis closes his eyes in ecstasy, like a Food Channel host telegraphing how great something tastes. He breathes, "Wow. That is insanely delicious. Just . . . wow." He opens his eyes and gazes at me with a look I've never seen in real life before. At least, not ever directed at me. He looks awestruck. I feel a flush all over. *Did it really work?*

"Thanks, Abby," he says earnestly. "You're an incredible baker."

He takes half a step toward the track and turns back to me. "Are you going to come out and watch my race? I'd really like that."

"I will," I tell Travis, and he smiles at me like the sun just came out.

When he trots away, Rachel and Kate are both staring at me.

"What did you . . ." Rachel starts.

Kate just says, "I want that recipe."

We run out of baked goods — including the rest of my undoctored cupcakes — before the meet's over. Kate is counting the money and Rachel and I are dumping loose crumbs out of Tupperware boxes when I hear the announcement for the high hurdles. That's Travis's event, the last race of the day.

"I want to go see this," I tell them both.

Rachel raises an eyebrow and asks, "Really?" and Kate says, "Hey, go for it."

I head for the track, where the team is already in starting position. The afternoon sun backlights Travis's hair as he assumes a crouch, his muscular legs coiled to spring from the gate. The starting gun sounds and he's airborne.

Could there be a better metaphor for Travis Brown than hurdling? Without breaking stride, he soars gracefully over each obstacle. That's how high school is for him, I think. Fun and effortless. It's never been like that for me — not for most people, I guess. But as I watch him leap, I feel like my heart's soaring with him. He's so far ahead of the pack that he crosses the finish line before the next runner has cleared the last hurdle.

I can't help it, I jump up and scream. The whole grandstand erupts into cheers. I see Megan jump out of her seat in a bright yellow dress that clings to her curves. She runs to embrace him, and I hold my breath. Here comes the moment of truth.

As Megan propels herself into his arms, Travis lifts her right off the ground. She covers his whole face with kisses.

My stomach and heart drop. Well, so much for *my* magic powers.

I'm about to head back to my car when I see Travis pull away from Megan, searching the bleachers. He's looking for . . . could it be *me*?

I stand very still, my nerves on edge.

Travis continues to gaze around, and then he spots me, standing just outside the chain-link fence. He smiles and waves. Megan follows his gaze, and when she sees that he's waving at me, her spine stiffens. Her hands fly to her hips, and she thrusts her chin and chest forward, sputtering something indignant at Travis.

Travis shrugs and says something short, which might be "So what?" Whatever it is, Megan turns on her heel and stalks off in a rage. And Travis does not look upset in the least — in fact, he looks delighted.

Wow. Just . . . wow.

Travis's teammates cluster around him, thumping him on the back and exclaiming about his win. I can't see him at all in the throng, but that's just as well, since I'm having some trouble with breathing.

Two thoughts are battling for space in my brain: *Did I really do that?* and *What's Megan going to do to me this time?* If I've gained her boyfriend's attention, that means I'll be poison to her. Suddenly, I worry I've made a terrible mistake.

I turn and walk blindly back to my car, feeling a swell of excitement and fear. I need to get out of here fast. As I turn my key in the ignition, I notice my gas gauge is almost at empty.

Perfect. Nothing like a dull, routine errand to slow down your galloping pulse rate.

I drive to the Mobil across from the mini-mall strip where Dad's computer shop sits next to a Dunkin' Donuts.

There you go, Abby, I think. *Back to normal. Fill up the tank with unleaded, and go treat yourself to a Boston Kreme. Life in the fast lane.*

I unscrew the gas cap and fill the tank, taking deep breaths as I watch the numbers click upward. By the time I go inside to pay Mr. Schneller, I've almost forgotten I've been casting hexes on track stars. Until I start back toward my car and see Travis's Alfa Romeo pull in right behind it.

"Hi, Abby," he says with a grin. "I *thought* that was your Jetta."

He's noticed what car I drive? I must look totally shocked. If somebody told me my mouth was wide open, I wouldn't blink. But it isn't. Some confident self that I don't even recognize seems to have taken over my body, stretching my lips into a relaxed, easy smile.

"Oh, hi," my voice says nonchalantly. "Small world."

"I'm so glad to see you," he says. No mention of winning his race at the track meet; he's not showing off. Which is kind of cool. Especially when he looks so terrific, his hair windswept, his face flushed from exercise. His arm is draped over the side of the door, and the hairs on his muscular forearm look golden.

"Want to go for a drive?" he asks me. He perches his sunglasses back on his forehead, and his blue eyes look right into mine. "Come on, it's convertible weather. Top down, get some wind in your hair . . . What do you say? You can leave your car here." And then he adds, "Please, Abby?"

Okay, now my inner jaw is dropped down to my toes, but my confident stand-in just makes me shrug and say, "Sure."

Travis heads north, toward the lighthouse at Newburyport. I'm very relieved that he didn't pick Salem for his scenic drive — seeing Rem when I'm with him would just make me feel confused, when I should be enjoying every moment.

Because this is really amazing.

The trees are in tender new leaf and the ocean is sparkling. It feels like a dream to be zipping along in Travis's little red sports car, with the stereo cranked and the road rushing by. My hair's blowing in front of my face; I must look like a tumbleweed. But I notice that people we drive past are waving at us with indulgent smiles, and I imagine them thinking we make a cute couple.

My heart gives a soft little flutter, like butterfly wings. It's hard to believe this is real, that I'm actually sitting here next to the boy I've been dreaming about for so long. It would be beyond perfect, except for one thing: Travis can't seem to stop complimenting me . . . or dissing Megan.

At first it's a pleasure to hear him praise me to the skies, even though I know it's the hex powder talking. It's still pretty swoony when someone who you've had a crush on for most of your life tells you over and over that you look beautiful.

"I mean it," he says. "You should always wear that shade of blue. It brings out your eyes. And your smile is amazing."

It's just the spell, I tell myself, but my heart pounds and I blush all the same.

Then he starts in on Megan — how selfish she is, how demanding and jealous. It also feels great to hear Travis complain about someone who's made me feel two inches tall all through high school. But after a while it starts getting uncomfortable. I try changing the subject — *Oh, look, there's a sailboat! Where did you find this adorable car? Did you break the school record for hurdles?* — but wherever the conversation may lead, it always loops back to how wonderful I am, how friendly and warm, and how totally different from Megan.

"Whenever I try to talk to her about anything going on with me, she zones out," Travis complains. "She wants all the focus on her. It just makes me so mad when she does that, you know?" He glances at me, and then back at the road. "It's like no one exists except her."

I nod. *This is all my fault*, I think, feeling more than a little bit guilty as we speed along the spectacular coast. Travis tilts his head, shooting me an appreciative glance. "You're a really good listener, you know?"

Yes, I am. And maybe a really good witch.

At dinner that night, Dad keeps looking at me over his plate of linguini. At first I think it's because of my wild windblown hair, but then he says, "Did I see you getting into a red convertible at the Mobil this afternoon?"

"Oh," I say, feeling my cheeks heat up. "Travis Brown gave me a ride after school, that's all."

Dad's eyebrows go up. He's never had to play the "protective" role because I never get asked out on dates. He seems to be a mix of concerned and pleased. He twirls a forkful of pasta against his spoon, dredging it through the

Bolognese sauce. Finally, he says, "Good athletes, those Brown kids. Fast runners." He looks at me. "Don't do anything you'll regret."

Good advice, Dad. You sound pretty fatherly.

Dad's not the only one who's reassessing my social status. The whole school is buzzing with rumors about Travis and Megan's big fight at the track meet. And a few people have heard that he likes some weird junior.

He certainly does. He's been following me like a puppy all day. He waited for me in the parking lot after Megan went in with her friends, walked me to my locker, and spent most of lunch sending me moony-eyed looks. It's exciting, but more than a little bit scary — I know Megan's gunning for me.

"You?" Rachel says at our after-school tutoring session at my house. "Is that who they're talking about?"

"Is that so hard to believe, that someone might like me?" I demand, feeling hurt.

"Not just *someone*. The alpha male of this admittedly limited herd. And another girl's boyfriend, P.S."

Rachel is looking at me with a blend of concern and disdain, as if I've fallen off the smart-nerd shelf and turned into Snooki. A very tall, very pale Snooki.

"I thought we were here to do trig," I say, bristling.

"Well, we would be," says Rachel, "if you'd done your homework. What's going on with you, Abby?"

More than you can imagine, I think. For a moment, I consider trying to tell her the whole thing — she is, after all, my closest friend now — but the idea of talking to practical, analytical Rachel Mendoza about magic spells is preposterous. She'd think I've gone out of my mind. And you know what? She might not be wrong.

I may not be doing my trig homework, but I have been studying. I've been poring over the spell book every night. The love potion worked so well that it's made me skittish about trying more, but I still want to find out what's possible. I just wish I had someone to share all this with.

For one split second in my room last night, I had considered calling up Valerie in Sarasota, and telling her everything — she might believe me. But then I remembered how far apart we've drifted. It would be so awkward to call her up and say, "Guess what? I'm a witch!"

"I don't know what to tell you," I finally say to Rachel. "This is just a weird time."

Rachel sighs, shutting her trigonometry textbook. "You want my diagnosis? One part end-of-the-year junioritis and one part hormones. The only thing I can't figure out is whether you're crushing on Travis or Rem."

That makes two of us.

When I go to Salem on Saturday morning, I stop by the Double Double Café to pick up a mocha. It's become my tradition — I've never been much of a coffee drinker, but now I relish the chance to see Rem every morning on my way to work. But Rem's not at the café today. I'm surprised by how disappointed I am. I order a coffee from Kara, the pretty barista with uptilted eyes and a tattooed black rose on her shoulder.

"Rem took a personal day," she says, handing me a double caramel mocha in a to-go cup.

"I didn't ask," I say, doing my best not to blush.

Kara's smile is wry. "You didn't have to."

Is she making fun of me, or sympathizing? Either way, I'm embarrassed. I drop all my change in the tip jar and leave very fast.

The weather's deliciously balmy all day. Dyami leaves the store's door propped open to usher in tourists. It's Memorial Day weekend, so they're out in force. We do a booming business in souvenir maps and books about everything from Nostradamus to pet massage. Dyami does tarot and palm readings practically nonstop, so I'm really busy at the cash register. When the customers need help finding something, I always know just where it is. I even give people advice about crystals and herbs. I'm starting to get really good at this job.

It's still warm outside when we close for the night. I ought to head home, but first I decide to unwind with an impulsive walk through a part of town I've never seen, out past the high school and power plant. It's a spit of land jutting between two coves, with short blocks of old, modest houses and several small churches. I know there's a park with a beach at the end, but I'm not sure how far. I'm walking past a ramshackle marina when some instinct tells me to cross the street and go inside the fence of its boatyard.

I swing the gate open and take a few tentative steps, looking around. What am I doing here?

A tan-armed boy is walking past me, his face hidden by the cooler he's carrying on his shoulder. He turns, and my pulse quickens.

It's Rem.

For the first time, he seems genuinely surprised to cross paths with me, and I can't help wondering if this time I'm the one who made the coincidence happen, just by wanting to see him so much. He looks great, of course. His T-shirt is damp and the cooler he's carrying smells of seawater.

"What is that?" I ask him.

"Dinner," says Rem. He sets down the cooler and lifts off the top. Inside is a silvery fish packed on ice, with a cluster of shrimp. "My friend's boat just came in. I helped them unload, and they gave me a tip."

"I thought you might be sick, since you weren't at —"

He cuts off my sentence. "I had some stuff to take care of, that's all." He's not meeting my eye, and for the first time since I've known him, he seems ill at ease. I have the sensation that he's hiding something. Then he flashes his usual dimply grin. "Want to join me for dinner?"

My heart leaps. I so wish I could, but I promised Matt I'd pick up takeout Chinese on my way back through Beverly, and it's already past six. "I wish. But I've got to get home. My family's expecting me."

"I'll take a rain check," says Rem. "Can you come see my place, at least? Since you're in my front yard?"

I look around. All I can see are a lot of old boats, a diesel pump, and a repair shed.

Rem notices my confusion and smiles. "You're looking right at it." He points at a vintage red tugboat tied up to the very last dock.

I feel my eyes widen. "You live on a *tugboat*?"

"I'm fixing it up. Come and see."

Rem leads me through a maze of boats up in dry-dock, their round hulls exposed like white whales. People are taking them out of storage for the summer, and I can smell fresh paint and varnish. A couple of seagulls flap skyward as we step onto the . . .

Oh. My. God. *Bridge.*

I can't help it, I grab Rem's arm. I've gotten used to crossing the Beverly Bay Bridge in my car, but this is a thin strip of floating wood with no railings at all, which bobs up and down on the water with each step we take. It's my personal nightmare.

Rem can't help but notice. I've gone white as a sheet and I'm digging my fingernails into his forearm.

"Abby?"

"I'm sorry, I'm kind of . . . I'm not good with bridges."

Rem sets down the cooler and pats it. "Step up."

"What? Onto that?"

"Go on, it'll hold you." He takes my hand, helping me up. As soon as I'm standing on top of the cooler, he turns around. In one swift motion, he lifts me onto his back.

The breath goes right out of my body. I can feel my heart beating against his strong back as my arms wrap around his chest, my cheek pressing into his brine-damp hair. Suddenly, the last thing I've got on my mind is the wobbly bridge. I want this to go on forever and ever.

Rem carries me piggyback all the way down to the tugboat. Then he sets me down, easing me onto its deck. He turns to face me, and I feel a magnetic charge crackle between us. He's looking into my eyes with a sudden intensity, as if he's trying to find out not just what I'm thinking, but who I *am*. The blue streak inside his green iris seems brighter than ever. I wonder if he sees the gold streak in my eye.

Neither one of us seems to be breathing. Is he going to kiss me? I've never been kissed, but I can almost imagine it — the feel of his lips on mine.

But no, this is Rem Anders, the king of mixed messages. Just when I think he's about to lean close and brush our lips together, he turns suddenly, breaking the moment.

"Come on, I'll show you around. Watch your head, the door's low."

I really don't get this. I wasn't imagining things; we were heartbeats away from kissing, and then he just turned off the switch. Travis would never pull this kind of mind game. He's been completely consistent with all his compliments — okay, maybe it's just because of a spell, but I know where I stand with him. Maybe I ought to bake Rem one of those special cupcakes.

But why do I get the feeling that magic cupcakes wouldn't work on Rem, that his will is much stronger than Travis's? That might be what makes him so hard to pin down. And so tantalizing.

Rem leads me across the deck, past a sea kayak he calls "my bike," and into the tug's living quarters. Some areas are freshly painted, some sanded and scraped, and some still covered in old, peeling paint. Next we head into the wheelhouse, where I'm surprised to see several unframed watercolors spread out to dry on the windowsill.

"Did you paint those?" I ask, pointing.

"Oh. Yeah. They're not finished. Just messing around."

I pick up a landscape with budding willow trees next to a creek. The quick sketch really catches the play of light over the water. "Rem, this is really good."

He looks embarrassed. "Something to do, right? What I really should paint is the kitchen. It's wicked funky down there. Can I make you some coffee? Though it's not double caramel mocha."

I smile. "That's okay. Will you be at the café tomorrow?"

"Of course." Rem looks at me. "You've got to go now, right?"

I nod. "I wish I didn't." He has no idea how much I mean that.

Or maybe he does. He looks at me with a flirtatious smile. "Do you need me to carry you back?"

I can feel myself blushing. "That would be . . . if you don't . . . Yes."

"Okay," says Rem. "But we're definitely going to work on this fear-of-bridges thing."

"I know, it's ridiculous. I just get this panicky feeling that I'm going to fall in and drown. I guess it's because I don't know how to swim."

Rem looks as if he just found out I'm missing both legs. "You can't *swim*?"

Now my cheeks are bright red. "Don't make fun of me, please. It's not like I haven't tried learning. I just plain don't float."

"Everyone floats," says Rem. "You need the right person to show you how, that's all. Have you got a swimsuit?"

My cheeks are getting even hotter. "For sunbathing, yeah."

"Bring it tomorrow. First lesson right after work." He looks at me with those hypnotic eyes, and I feel my heart beat a little bit faster.

Who could say no?

Chapter 9

THERE'S NOTHING QUITE AS EXCRUCIATING as wearing a swimsuit in front of a guy you like. Especially when he's tawny and sun-kissed from working outdoors, and you look like a glass of skim milk.

I still have the sky blue bikini I picked up two summers ago for a beach party Valerie dragged me to. (I read a book in my beach chair the whole time, and nobody noticed I never got wet.) I don't know whether to be pleased or depressed that it still fits me perfectly. Not many new curves to show off, but I do have long legs, thanks to Mom.

On Saturday night, I stand in front of my bedroom mirror in the bikini, frowning at my reflection. Here's the deal: tall, thin, and fair-skinned is not going to change. What's the difference between regal, slender, and elegant (think Nicole Kidman or Taylor Swift) and gawky, skinny, and pale (Abby Silva)? Is it posture, self-confidence, star power? Whatever it is, I've got till tomorrow at five to channel my version, or I'm going to be too self-conscious to live.

Rem meets me in front of Spiral Visions, and I see that he's carrying a canvas tote bag and two towels.

"Do you need to change?" he asks, his eyes roaming over my neckline for telltale bikini straps. I wish I could stop myself from blushing again.

"Doesn't the park beach have dressing rooms?" I ask.

"They're not open till June twenty-first. Anyway, we're not swimming there. There's no lifeguard on duty, and I thought you would want to go someplace more private."

I swallow. *So I can make a fool of myself in front of just you?*

Well, I suppose it is better than every dog-walker, Frisbee-tosser, and kid on the swings saying, "What? You can't *swim*?"

I can't wait until this is over.

The first thing I notice when we park next to Rem's secret cove is the willows. They are the same ones from his painting, their yellow-green fronds dangling into a creek. *Willowy*, there's the word I was looking for. I'm not tall and gawky, I'm *willowy*.

Right.

Rem leads me down a short, packed-dirt trail to the spot where the creek meets salt water. The sand looks like hard-packed brown sugar. There's a flat rock that's perfect for sunning or picnicking — all the sane things a person can do near the water. But we're actually going *in*.

Rem sets down the tote bag and towels, kicks off his shoes, and wades right into the mouth of the creek, which, I'm relieved to see, only comes up to his ankles. He smiles, wiggling his toes.

"Getting warmer," he says. "Not bad for Memorial Day."

He comes back out and shucks off his T-shirt and cargo shorts, tossing them on the flat rock. He looks great in his swim trunks, as I knew he would. The tan wedge of his chest tapers into a lean belly, just washboard enough to turn my cheeks warm. The glow of late-afternoon sun makes his skin look like butterscotch.

My turn. I step out of my sandals, take a deep breath, and pull my dress over my head, exposing my sky blue bikini and pale, skinny — make that *willowy* — torso. Rem doesn't look disappointed, which is awfully nice of him. Without taking his eyes off mine, he walks backward into the creek, and holds out his hand.

I can do this, I tell myself. If I can move traffic cones, make candles relight, and mix up a love potion that works,

I can stand up with my feet in the water. Especially if I get to hold hands with Rem.

I walk to the edge of the creek. He smiles at me, taking my hand, and I dip one foot into the water. It's so cold I practically shout.

"This is *warmer*?" I stutter. "Warmer than what, Glacier Bay?"

"You get used to it." Rem's smile is encouraging. He squeezes my hand, taking a step backward into the water. Then he reaches for my other hand. I follow him, carefully placing one foot in front of the other. Soon we're facing each other in ankle-deep water.

"That's not so bad, is it?" he asks with a twinkle.

It's actually not bad at all, except for my feet feeling practically numb. And how much I wish Rem would lean forward and kiss me.

"Aren't your feet freezing?" I ask him.

"I'm used to cold water. I go kayaking all year long," he says with a shrug. "You're just cold because you're not moving. Stay right there." He splashes back out to the rock. There, he takes an old portable CD player out of his tote bag, and presses the Play button.

I have to admit the last thing I expected to hear blasting into a secluded cove on the far end of Salem was "Teach

Me How to Dougie." Rem busts a dance move and I burst out laughing.

"Don't you like to Dougie?" He grins. "I burned you a mix."

"Of course. But it's, I don't know, it's so goofy to —"

"Don't think about it. Just warm yourself up." He steps back into the creek and starts dancing for real, with great style and silliness. Laughing, I join him.

Rem is an energetic, playful dancer. Splashing and kicking, we both let loose, working our way backward into the shallow cove. When the song ends, I'm shocked to discover I'm hip-deep in salt water and not even scared.

"Having fun?" Rem asks, and I nod eagerly. Then the next song begins. It's a ballad, just right for a slow dance, and I feel my breath catch. The sun hovers over Rem's shoulder, illuminating his thatch of dark hair and catching me full in the face. I can feel myself squinting against the bright light, but before I can turn, Rem raises one hand toward my cheekbone.

"I can see it," he murmurs. "The fire in your eyes."

I hold my breath.

He brushes his fingertips over my skin.

"That ought to chase off the chills," he says, and I realize that he's right, that a glow like warm honey is spreading all through my veins. Is it Rem's touch that released it, or something inside me? Our faces are inches apart, and he's gazing right into my eyes. My lips part. If this were a movie, the sound track would swell for our first kiss.

But that's not what happens at all. Rem's eyes flood with sadness, and he takes a sudden step backward. He slowly, reluctantly drops his hands. Is it my newfound confidence that makes me think he doesn't actually want to let go of me?

"We better head home," he says.

"Now?" I blurt out before I can cover my deep disappointment. "But what about my swimming lesson?"

Rem smiles. "That *was* your first lesson."

All the way home, I keep going over those moments in the water. Rem running hot and cold is nothing new: He's been like that as long as I've known him. Sometimes he seems to be coming on strong, as attracted to me as I am to him. And then there are times when I feel him pull back, as if something inside him is telling him he shouldn't let himself do this. The question is why.

There's a lot about Rem that's mysterious. Does he live by himself on that tugboat? Where is his family? And why do I sometimes feel as if I can hear his voice inside my head, and other times feel I don't know him at all?

One thing I do know for sure: Rem is a mystery I want to solve. Especially after I find out that he's tucked the sketch I liked inside my purse — he must have put it there while I was pulling my dress back on over my swimsuit after our lesson.

When I get home, I hang the painting up next to my bedroom mirror. He gave me a present. A present he made with his own hands. That's got to mean *something*, right?

Later that night, instead of my usual shower, I light candles all over the bathroom, pour a capful of perfumed soap under the tap, and lower myself into a hot bath in the old claw-foot tub. The water comes up to my chin, and the scent is delicious, like night-blooming jasmine.

I lie there surrounded by bubbles, reviewing the day in my head. I see Rem peel his white T-shirt over his head, exposing his smooth, muscled chest; feel him squeezing my hand as he coaxes me into the water. I see the two of us dancing and splashing, enjoying the music and having a great time together. I feel the warm touch of his finger tracing my face as he tells me that he sees the fire in my eyes. It all feels like a dream, something that would happen to somebody else, not to me. I close my eyes, feeling weightless as I let the water surround my whole body.

Wait. Am I . . . floating?

Something is definitely changing in me, and it's happening fast. I notice the way other kids at school look at me now, and it's not just surprise that I've let my wild hair out of its rubber band. It's as if I've moved out of the background and onto center stage; I can't disappear into the crowd anymore. People know who I am, like they know Samson Hobby and Makayla Graf.

Or Travis.

On Tuesday morning, he comes up behind me when I'm at my locker.

"Hey, Abby," he says softly. "You look really pretty today. Would you want to go for another drive sometime? I really like talking to you."

Well, of course you do, I want to say. *I've won your attention.*

"That would be really nice," I say instead. It still seems surreal to be talking to my secret crush in the clear light of day. It's like having your daydream come true. But that was also how I felt about my swimming lesson with Rem — and that didn't involve any spell books or potion-laced cupcakes.

"I've got track practice after school," he says. "Maybe this weekend?"

"I work on the weekends," I tell him. "But soon."

Travis smiles. "I'll look forward to that." He starts walking away, then turns back, rocking onto his heels. "Maybe you could bake some of those coconut cupcakes. Those were out of this world."

Good choice of words, I think, smiling and nodding. I almost feel sorry for him as I watch him bounce off down the hall, stretching up to tap his fingers on a lighting fixture as if it's a basketball rim. He really is awfully cute.

At lunch the next day, I watch several girls from the Social Committee taping up posters for senior prom. It's happening on June 21, and tickets are on sale now. The whole cafeteria's buzzing with gossip about who's going with whom. I can't help remembering the way Megan waltzed into Spiral Visions and shelled out for that crystal necklace. I'm glad she's got a heart made of quartz, because she certainly doesn't seem to have Travis's heart anymore.

In the cafeteria, he's sitting with some of his track team buddies, and keeps looking longingly at the table where I'm eating with Kate, Rachel, and Rachel's friend Vijay Sahasrabudhe, a tall, skinny math whiz with Buddy Holly–style glasses. I've always suspected that Vijay likes Rachel, but she blushes and waves me off whenever I bring up the topic.

"Travis totally likes you," Kate tells me now. "He's been grinning at you ever since that day at the bake sale."

"The question is whether our Abby reciprocates," Rachel says. "I'd like to think she has better taste."

"Have you ever hung out with him?" Kate asks. "He's a really sweet guy. He does all these charity fund-raiser runs for cancer research and stuff like that. It's not his fault he looks like a Hollister ad. I think you should go for it, Abby."

"Isn't he still dating Megan Kardashian?" Vijay asks, and Rachel and Kate snort with laughter.

"Yes," Rachel says. "So how sweet can he be?"

I laugh, enjoying the fact that nobody at this table is a fan of Megan. It's funny how someone can get to be popular when most people don't seem to like them at all. Vijay isn't the first guy I've heard who shares my opinion of Megan: In history class the other day, Samson Hobby called her Toxic Barbie, and nicknamed her sidekicks Clamber and Clone. "I can't wait till they graduate," he'd added, a welcome reminder that in less than a month, Megan Keith will be out of my life.

But not yet. In fact, there she is now, coming off the hot lunch line with Amber and Sloane. She's heading toward Travis's table, but as soon as she sees that he's smiling at me, and I'm laughing, she swivels and starts walking straight toward me. Amber and Sloane follow in wedge formation, like a couple of very short bodyguards. I can hear their heels click-clacking on the linoleum.

Megan stops right in front of me. She's wearing a hot-pink V-neck T-shirt and a white skirt the approximate texture and size of a washcloth.

"What's so funny?" she asks me.

"Private joke," I say, which is sort of the truth.

Not the answer she wanted, though. She leans into my face, her eyes flashing with spite. "If I ever hear that you set foot in Travis's car again, I will ruin your life. He's *my* boyfriend. Not yours."

A couple of weeks ago, Megan's threats filled me with dread. But now I just look at this spiteful and jealous girl, who's secretly terrified she's not the superstar that she wants everybody to think she is.

You can't ruin my life, I tell her silently. *You don't have that power.*

And right behind that is a scarier thought: I *do* have that power.

I watch as Megan stalks off with Clamber and Clone, clearly disappointed she hasn't rattled me. Travis is still watching me from across the room with a smile.

I've dethroned the queen of the monkeys. But here's the ironic thing: Now that her boyfriend, my lifelong secret crush and the boy of my dreams, is getting obsessed with me, my heart's drifting elsewhere. To Rem Anders, who won't ever give me a straight yes or no, and is always just out of my reach.

What is the cruel kink in our wiring that always seems to make the person you *can't* have glow so much brighter than someone who actually wants you? If I had a potion to unravel that age-old mystery, it would be worth more than gold.

As the week goes on, Travis continues to dote on me, waiting for me at my locker and complimenting whatever I'm wearing. He keeps asking me if I'll bake something for him. It gets to the point where I actually try to avoid seeing him in the halls. I can't wait to get back to Salem and my next swimming lesson with Rem. Maybe we'll actually make it all the way into the water this time. And maybe he'll finally kiss me. It's hard to say which would be more unbelievable.

My classes float past in a careless blur. I can't focus on anything my teachers are saying. I'm barely keeping up with my homework, much less cramming for final exams, but somehow I still get straight A's on every review sheet and prep quiz. The less effort I put into studying, the better I do. I'm starting to suspect that my witchy talents extend beyond potions and over to test-taking. Somehow I always intuit the right way to solve a trigonometry problem or which one of the multiple choice circles I should fill in. The right answer seems to glow under my fingers, the way certain stones did in Dyami's bins. Maybe I should sign up to retake my SATs. Do magical powers count as cheating, or just as good luck?

Rachel has no patience with my new attitude. "You can't keep on slacking like this," she says when I meet her at her locker to tell her I'm going to skip our next tutoring session in the library. "You're a *junior*. This is the transcript year colleges look at. It's when everything matters the most. And your trig final's coming up soon."

"My grades are just fine," I retort, annoyed.

"But you're not even doing your homework. Sooner or later, it's going to come back to bite you."

I shrug. Why is she riding me like this? She sounds like a nagging parent. "When there's a problem, I'll fix it, okay?"

"You know what, Abby? There *is* a problem," says Rachel. I swallow hard, feeling a pit in my stomach as she plows on. "You never have time for me anymore. I can't remember when we last hung out together. Oh, yes, I can. I do remember. The day I helped you get your license, and instead of going to Chinatown afterward, like we'd been planning for weeks, you insisted on going to Salem. And signed up for a job in that wacko gift shop, and turned into someone I don't even recognize."

Wow. She's really been storing this up.

Rachel's waiting for me to say something. I don't know what to tell her. It's true that I'm changing, a lot, but I can't tell her why. I just can't.

And I guess my big secret has blasted a hole in our friendship, because she gives a bitter nod, and says, "Fine. You want me to leave you alone? I can do that." She packs up her books and storms away from me, down the hall.

I stand with my heart beating hard, watching her go. My closest friend is clearly furious at me. That hurts, but it also makes me mad at *her*. I feel really judged. Rachel's neat little world of overachieving and honors and high SAT scores seems like another old skin that I've shed. There's more to life than being the valedictorian. I think even Rachel knows that.

So maybe she's not really mad at me. Maybe she's envious. Maybe deep down in her heart of hearts, Rachel Mendoza is wishing that someone like Travis or Rem would start looking at *her*.

I could mix her a potion for that, but I don't think she'd let me.   .

Chapter 10

SATURDAY FINALLY COMES, AND WITH IT my next swimming lesson. The sun's dipping low as Rem brings me back to the sheltered cove. This time we don't dance, but walk hand in hand into the water.

"We've got all the time in the world," he says, twining his fingers through mine. "You tell me when."

I nod. The water does seem a little bit warmer this time, or maybe it's me. With each step, it rises a little bit higher, and so does my anxiety level. When the water comes up to my hips, I hesitate.

Rem stops at once. "Little pause?"

"You must think I'm such a wimp."

"I think you're great," he says, and my heart skips a beat. Rem turns to face me, resting his free hand on my side, just above my waist. "This is where we need to get you. So here's my proposal. For every step we take, we'll tell each other something about ourselves."

What is this, some kind of truth or dare? As if I don't feel exposed enough wearing a bikini and — hello! — learning to *swim*.

"Like what?" I ask, trying to keep my voice neutral.

"Anything," Rem says. "My favorite flavor of ice cream is butter pecan."

"Wow, that's revealing," I say with a smile. "Mine is rocky road."

"Cool," says Rem, taking a tiny step backward and bringing me with him, as if we were dancing a waltz. "I used to play the trombone in the middle school band."

"Clarinet," I say. "But I really stunk."

Now it's Rem's turn to smile. "So did I." He takes a step backward, and I feel the water slide up past the hem of my bikini bottom.

"I was the tallest kid in my class every year till ninth grade," I say.

"I was the wildest. I got sent to the principal's office every two days. My mom called me Rembo."

"My mom died when I was eleven." Wow. I didn't think I would tell him *that*. The water is up to my navel, and I can't help shivering.

"I'm so sorry," says Rem. "Do you want to stop for a minute?"

I shake my head. *No*, I think. *I want to tell you everything*. And out it spills. Stuff about growing up. About Dad and Matt and my Portuguese cousins, and feeling like some kind of freak at family gatherings. How much I miss Mom. Things I haven't told anyone, not even Valerie or Rachel.

He tells me about being half-Abenaki, how his French-Canadian relatives call him an Indian and his Native American relatives call him "white boy with a feather." That he bought the tugboat at a salvage auction with money he'd saved up for college. That his temperamental dad kicked him out of the house. They've made up, and Rem goes home to visit, but he wants to prove he can live on his own, on his tugboat. That he loves to paint, but worries he'll never be good enough.

I don't remember us moving, but somehow we've edged into much deeper water. There's a trace of a smile on Rem's lips, just enough for his dimples to indent his cheeks.

"Look where you are," he says.

I turn and glance over my shoulder. The flat rock where we left our clothes seems so far away. I'm surrounded by water, and I'm not freaked out. This is huge.

"How are you doing?" Rem asks me.

"I'm fine," I tell him, and it's true.

"You ready to try floating?" Rem asks. "If I hold you?"

I look at his green-and-blue eyes reflecting the colors of water. If Rem asked me right now if I'd like to try jumping out of a plane, I'd say yes if he offered to hold me.

"Sure thing," I tell him.

"Put your arms around my neck," he says. "Keep your eyes on mine."

Oh, that is so not a problem.

There's a hum of excitement gathering under my skin as our eyes lock and hold. Drawing in a breath, I wrap my wet arms around his neck, feeling as if my whole life is about to change.

"I'm going to pick you up now, okay?" he says. "Feet off the ground."

I nod, and in one fluid twist, Rem dips one arm under my knees, lifting me up in the classic over-the-threshold position. Except that he's up to his chest in the ocean. And so am I.

"You're up," he says. "How does it feel?"

Dreamy. Amazing. "I'm fine," I say. "But I'm not floating."

Rem grins. "Not *yet*. But if you're in a hurry . . ."

"I'm not," I say quickly. "I'm fine just like this." *In fact, I could do it all day.*

"I think you're ready," he says. "So what you're going to do is stretch out flat on your back, lying across my arms. Think magician's assistant."

I hesitate. Flat on my back? No more arms around his neck, no more eye contact? *Please*, I think, *don't make me do this.*

You can, says the look in Rem's eyes. Reluctantly I let go of his neck and try to lie flat with my hands at my sides. I can feel myself tensing up. Then I hear Rem's voice in my head: *It's all right. I've got you.*

He does, in all ways. His arms are outstretched underneath me, holding me up, and I feel my anxiety starting to melt away. Until he starts to lower his arms.

The second I feel him let go, I seize up in a panic, thrashing and sputtering. Rem's arms come right back underneath me.

"You're okay, Abby," he says. "I've got you. You're safe."

"I'm sorry," I gasp, clinging onto his neck.

"No, I'm sorry. Really. I didn't mean to . . . I'll take you back in, okay?"

I nod, feeling like an idiot. Couldn't I just have been chill for two seconds? Why do I have to be so crazy?

Rem carries me back toward the shore. "I should have told you I was about to let go. I thought if you weren't anticipating it, you'd be less tense."

"It wouldn't have made any difference," I tell him. "I can't float."

"The thing is, you *did* float. You just didn't know you were floating."

It's shallow enough now for me to start walking. As soon as the evening air hits my wet skin, I start to shiver uncontrollably. Rem sees and splashes ahead, coming back with a beach towel, which he wraps around me. Then he takes me in his arms, towel and all.

"I'm so sorry," he murmurs, holding me close.

"It isn't your fault. I have awful nightmares sometimes, about drowning," I tell him. "They're set in the past, but they feel absolutely real, as if they're not dreams but memories. I can see every detail, feel my mouth and lungs filling with water."

"It's no wonder you don't want to swim," Rem says.

I look into his eyes. The wedge of blue inside the green seems especially bright, like a sliver of seawater.

"Sometimes you're in them," I blurt. "Or . . . or someone whose eyes look exactly like yours."

Why did I say that?

I want to splash back into the water and lower myself under. Anything to stop this embarrassment warming my face.

But Rem nods, as if he's not surprised in the least. And then I open my mouth and I just keep spilling, about all the weird things that have been happening to me. I tell him how I read about Sarah and Dorcas Good, and the traffic cone, and all the spooky coincidences. I tell him about the spell book, and the candles. The only thing I don't reveal is the love potion and Travis.

"I know this sounds insane," I finish, "but I think I might really have . . . magical powers."

It's the first time I've said the words out loud, and they feel all too real.

Rem shakes his head, his mood darkening suddenly, as if a storm just rolled in off the ocean. "It doesn't sound crazy" is all he says.

I don't know what makes me so bold, but I've said too much to stop now.

"Do you have them, too?" I ask. "I mean, sometimes you just seem to *know* things, and sometimes I think I can hear you —"

Stop, Abby.

"Like that," I say. "I just heard your voice inside my head. Does that mean —"

Not now. Rem's eyes fix on mine, urgent and fearful. *Not here and not now.*

"But —"

Rem shakes his head. "I think you're imagining things," he says brusquely. He splashes to shore and grabs up his things. "Come on, let's get out of here."

All the way home I keep kicking myself. How could I have told Rem that I heard his voice inside my head, or saw his eyes in my dreams? He must think I'm a four-alarm nut case. What on earth was I thinking? I even told him I had magical powers. I've had enough sense not to blurt that to Rachel, so why would I open my mouth up to someone I barely know but am falling for, harder and harder?

The sun's gone below the horizon, and my headlights sweep over the road as I follow the turns to my neighborhood. Back to the dull and predictable life that I don't seem to fit into at all anymore.

The second I park in our driveway, I know I'm in trouble. Dad flips on the exterior lights and stands framed in the doorway, arms folded across his chest. With an instantaneous wince, I remember that he had a date with Danielle tonight, and I was supposed to come straight home from work to watch Matt. The I-messed-up calculus clicks through my brain: Can I make up a plausible story, or should I just own up to my mistake? Will it make things better or worse if I tell him the truth: I forgot?

"Where have you been?" he demands when I reach him.

"I am so sorry," I say. "I lost track of time."

"We've been planning this dinner all week. I reminded you yesterday. And why didn't you have your phone on? I called you five times and kept getting your voice mail."

That's because I was trying to swim in the *ocean*. With somebody *I'd* like to go on a dinner date with. But Dad isn't finished.

"I reserved us a table at Le Canard and we had to cancel. Do you know how hard it is for Danielle to get Saturday nights off?"

How in the world would I know that, and why would I care? But however I might feel about her, it *was* my mistake.

"I'm so sorry, Dad," I say. "I totally blew it. I owe you one."

"Yes, you do," Dad says. "How about right now?"

I didn't expect that, but I can hardly refuse. Especially when Danielle appears from inside the house and comes up beside him, slipping her arm through his.

"That is so sweet of you, Joe," she says, smiling at him. "Thanks so much, Abby."

What can I possibly say? *Get your arm off my father, stop dyeing your hair, don't pretend that you like me?* I opt for silence instead.

You should have told me that she was still here, I think, fuming inside as Dad pats her charm-braceleted hand.

I can't help it. I don't like this woman, I don't want her dating my dad, and I'm not going to stand here and fake it. If she sees the resentment that burns in my eyes, so be it.

The first thing I see are the torches, dripping with tar, held high aloft by a noisy mob. They've tied me to a pole with my hands bound behind me, so tight I can't move. My hair's been shorn close to the scalp with a knife that's left nicks on raw skin. I feel splintery wood underneath my bare feet. Fear courses through me, an animal thing. I can smell my own sweat.

I see them come closer, their faces twisted and cruel in the flickering torchlight. Someone holds a torch to a pile of dry tinder, and flames start dancing around my feet, sending up cinders and ash. All at once there's a whoosh *as the fire is engaged. Hot smoke fills my lungs as the wood pile I'm standing on bursts into flame. I can smell my own skin, singed and crackling. The pain is so sharp that I think I'll split open. A wild cry escapes from my lungs, like the howl of a wolf, like a siren . . .*

A siren.

I slam out of sleep, drenched in panic and sweat, and the first thing I see is red flames on my ceiling. It takes me a second to register that the flashes of red come from the emergency lights of a fire truck speeding past my window, and that the siren I thought I was dreaming is real.

My heart is still racing. The passing siren wails into the distance, its pitch getting lower as it races toward some other neighborhood. I must have heard the loud sound in my sleep and worked it right into that hideous nightmare.

I sit up in bed, trying to shake off the spell that the dream cast.

My skin isn't burning. I'm not breathing smoke. Nothing is wrong, except for the images inside my head. And those won't go away. Not now, and not ever.

I haul myself into the bathroom to splash cold water on my face, passing the door to Matt's bedroom, where he lies fast asleep in the glow of his night-light, dreaming the dreams of the normal. *You don't know how lucky you are*, I think bitterly.

I go back to bed and somehow manage to fall back asleep. I finally sleep soundly, but I come downstairs in the morning feeling like something is . . . off.

I'm astonished to find Dad and Danielle huddling in our kitchen. They're both drinking black coffee, and she's wearing a T-shirt and jeans with no makeup or jewelry. She looks tense and worn out. If it weren't for her red hair, I'd think she was somebody else.

Then I notice the suitcase and Hefty bags full of clothes on the floor, along with some cartons of photographs, papers, and kitchen things.

"Dad?" I ask, bewildered. "What happened?"

He looks at me, grim-faced. "Danielle had a fire in her kitchen last night."

What?

"A fire?" I stammer. Now that he says it, I realize there's a distinct smell of smoke in the room. It must be from her clothes.

I'm sure I look white as a ghost, because Dad does his best to be reassuring. "Danielle's fine. The smoke detectors went off, and she got out in plenty of time. But her house is a mess, and she has to deal with insurance, and water damage, and —"

"All my stuff," Danielle says. She looks shell-shocked. "The firemen broke all my windows."

"She's going to be staying with us for a while," Dad says, taking her hand. Danielle starts to sob.

"Thank god you're here, Joe," she says to him. "I can't believe this."

Neither can I.

Chapter 11

IT WASN'T MY FAULT. THAT'S WHAT I KEEP trying to tell myself as I shower and dress that morning. The fire began when some paper bags Danielle had stored next to the fridge were ignited by an electrical spark from its plug. That's what the fire chief told her and Dad, but it doesn't help. What caused the electrical spark?

You can call it coincidence, but the first time I met Danielle, the sleeve of her blouse caught on fire. Did last night's fire siren set off the dream in my head, or was it the other way around?

What if the dreams in my head set the fire in Danielle's house?

If this is what being a witch is like, I don't want any part of it. I could have hurt her. Or Dad, when he went back to get her. That thought is a punch to the gut.

Can you turn your back on your magical powers? I

have no idea, but I'm going to try. I've done nothing but make other people unhappy. I've turned Rachel against me, made Rem think I'm crazy, and possibly burned down my dad's girlfriend's house. Yes, I've got Travis's attention, but now I'm not even sure I want it. And I certainly don't want the cruel attention of his scorned girlfriend.

The whole thing is a train wreck.

I'm already way late for work, but I've got to make one extra stop, at the Salem Library. I pull up in front of it just as the desk clerk comes outside to unlock the overnight book drop box. Perfect.

"I'd like to return this," I tell her, pulling the velvet-wrapped book from my purse. "I think it might be overdue."

She takes the book, turning it over to look at the spine. "This didn't come from our collection."

"It must have. I got it here just a few weeks ago, when I was doing research."

She shakes her head. "There's no card catalog number. And we don't stock handwritten books. Though I'm sure our historian would love to see this one. It looks very old."

"Can you give it to him?" There's a desperate edge in my voice.

"She doesn't come in on Sundays," the desk clerk says, handing the book back to me. "Come back next week. Ask for Mrs. Brinnier."

"But I don't want to . . . Never mind. Thanks." I walk back to my car, shoving the spell book back into my purse.

If it's not from the library, how did it get on the shelf? Or wind up in my bag after I put it back? I don't understand any of this.

I need to clear my head, and what I want most of all is to see Rem. I decide I'll get my morning mocha, and talk to him. Then, maybe things might begin to make sense again. I just hope he still wants to talk to me after all the craziness I revealed at our last swimming lesson.

Somehow (I refuse to think the word *magically*), I find a parking place right in front of the alley. It's the exact same spot where Rachel and I parked the first time I met Rem. As I get out of my car, my attention is drawn to two figures partway up the alley, leaning against the back door of the Double Double Café. It's a boy and a girl, and they're kissing.

The first thing I notice is the black rose tattoo on Kara's shoulder. Then she moves her arm and I see who she's kissing. My heart stops.

It's Rem.

I stand stock-still as the image sears into my brain. I feel as if three knives are stabbing me right through the heart. How could I have been so blind? It's been right under my nose this whole time, and I totally missed it. No wonder Rem has been acting so hot and cold with me!

They're so lost in each other they don't even notice I'm there. I stomp past the alley and slam the door into the store, where Dyami looks up, startled. You don't have to be a psychic to see something's wrong; it's written all over my face. But she's wise and respectful enough just to note it and not ask me questions. For that I am grateful.

Dyami sends me back to the stockroom to move stacks of cartons, and I throw myself into the boring, repetitive task while my mind races furiously.

I have been such a fool. Whatever made me think Rem would be interested in me? Kara is gorgeous. She lives right in Salem; they work at the same place. They've probably been dating since high school. So why in the world was he flirting with me?

And he totally was. Carrying me to his tugboat, teaching me how to swim, giving me one of his *paintings*? What was that about?

What a jerk. Just another cute guy who enjoys the ego boost of girls having crushes on him. I'm probably one of a long, long string. No wonder Kara gave me that smile the other day, when she made me that double caramel mocha. Rem is a player.

I slam another box onto the shelf, my sides heaving. I'm so mad I could throttle him. If I have the power to make bad things happen to people, Rem Anders is top of the list. Bring it on. He is toast.

The dark cloud of my mood doesn't lighten all day. When I drive back over the bridge to Beverly, heading into the sunset with Salem no more than a speck in my rearview mirror, all I can think is *good riddance*. I'm tempted to roll down the window and hurl the spell book right over the railing. Drown the sucker for good. If there wasn't a cop car right behind me, I'd do it.

Or maybe I wouldn't. You never know when you might want revenge on somebody.

Like Rem.

There's a red car next to Dad's in our driveway. It must be Danielle's. Not even the reminder of yesterday's fire at her house puts a lid on my anger. She has moved in overnight. The guest room is filled with her things, and she's colonizing the rest of the house, draping a fringed silk scarf over the sofa in place of my grandmother's afghan, and mixing her pots and pans in with ours in the kitchen. The whole house smells like garlic and beef.

She's making us dinner. That's *my* job.

"Abby?" she calls as I storm up the stairs. "Is that you?"

Busted. There's no way to avoid this.

"I'll be down in a second," I call back. I open the door

to my room, toss my purse onto the bed, and storm back downstairs in a sulk. Might as well get this over with.

When I enter the kitchen, Dad and Matt are both sitting down at the table. It's already set, with a tablecloth I've never seen before. There's a big tossed salad right in the center, along with a bottle of ranch dressing (Dad and Matt's favorite) and balsamic vinaigrette (mine). Has Danielle been researching us?

Calm down, I tell myself. *They were both in the fridge.*

Danielle's wearing my quilted oven mitts. She takes out a casserole dish and carries it to the table, setting it down on a trivet. It's full of meat loaf topped with ketchup and bubbling cheese.

"Careful, it's hot," she says as Matt leans forward to look.

"Mmm, that smells great," says Dad.

"I'm glad," says Danielle. She takes a foil-wrapped loaf of garlic bread out of the oven, twists it into a waiting basket, and hands it to him.

And I realize with a jolt that she's going to sit in Mom's chair.

"May I be excused?" I say, getting up before anybody can answer and beating a hasty retreat back upstairs to my room. I slam the door shut behind me and throw myself onto the bed. I wish I could cry, but I can't. It's as if I've boiled dry.

I don't know how long I lie there, facedown on the bedspread, but the first thing I see when I pick up my head is Rem's watercolor of the cove where he took me to swim. My fury redoubles. As I tear it down off the wall and crumple it up in one hand, I catch sight of my face in the mirror. My eyes are a thundercloud gray, and the gold rims seem to pulsate. The yellow-gold stripe across my left eye is the brightest it's ever been. I look possessed.

I rip open the drawer where I keep my candles, light one, and hold Rem's painting over it, watching it curl up and burn into ashes.

I stare at the candle. Could I cast a spell to make Rem lose interest in Kara? I probably could, but would I even want to? If he's the kind of guy who two-times his girlfriend and was just using my affections to make himself feel good, I don't care how handsome or charming he is. At least Travis Brown is *nice*. And he's crazy about me, no small thanks to my potion. If I gave him a bit more encouragement, he'd probably break up with Megan and ask me out.

An idea begins to take hold. Maybe it's good that I didn't return the green spell book to the library. Maybe this is my destiny. I never asked to have magical powers. I wasn't given a choice about this, any more than I was given a choice about losing my mother, or nightmares and headaches, or being that tall, gawky, weird girl who nobody likes.

Nobody except Travis Brown. And now I'm going to make him like me even more.

I open the spell book. The spidery handwriting no longer seems so off-putting. It's almost as if I can hear the voice of the woman who wrote this with her scratchy quill pen, whispering to me across the centuries. The book isn't signed, but I'm certain the person who gathered these herbs and magical objects, and wrote down these strange incantations, was somebody like me. I picture her young, thin, and pale, with a rim of gold fire in her eyes. I wonder if she was my actual ancestor, Sarah or Dorcas or one of her daughters. Whoever she was, she's my guide.

The potion I choose is called "To Inspire Deep and Abiding Love."

That's what I want, I realize. Not Rem's on-and-off-switch flirtations, not Travis's moonstruck stares and the empty compliments fueled by my starter potion. I want genuine, shared, lasting love. No more baby steps. If I've got this power, I want the real thing.

As I read over the spell, I'm relieved I don't have to sneak this potion into Travis's food. I don't want to have to bake something else and share my kitchen with Danielle.

I just have to put a pinch of the mixture under my tongue when his eyes are on me, and the spell will be cast.

The potion has just three ingredients:

Powdered Rose Petals
Essence of Jasmine
Wild Honeycomb

It's interesting that the more powerful love potion is so much simpler than the initial one for gaining affection. Maybe the spell imitates life: Crushes and flirtations can twist and turn in elaborate patterns, but I've always heard that when true love strikes, you just *know*.

That's what I need now. That unbending certainty.

Even if it has to come from a spell.

I wait until everyone else in the house is asleep. Then I mix the three ingredients in a silver spoon and light my seven candles. The spell book instructs:

Concentrate on thy Beloved with a Full Heart,
Releasing a Deep and Abiding Love.
What is Given, Shall Be Returned.

I close my eyes and picture Travis leaping over hurdles. I push out any images of Rem, and let my heart fill with thoughts of Travis — our friendship on the playground. Our afternoon drive. His smile.

Let him see me with new eyes, I think. *Not just skin-deep*

infatuation, but deep and abiding love, an emotion that spends its life buried and waiting to bloom.

I open my eyes. The flames rise up at once as I recite the final phrase of the incantation aloud:

"Goddess of Love, make it so."

The next morning I drive to school early and park next to the spot where Travis always leaves his red convertible. When I see him drive up, with the breeze riffling his golden hair, my heart does a little somersault.

Who needs Rem, anyway?

I get out and walk toward Travis's car. I'm wearing gold filigreed earrings I bought from Dyami and the same sky blue sundress Travis told me looked great with my coloring. So I'm feeling as close to confident as I'll ever get. Especially since I've got a pinch of true love potion tucked between my thumb and forefinger.

"Oh, hi, Travis," I say, trying to sound both off-handed and pleased to run into him. My heart's beating faster than usual. Maybe it did fill with love last night. He gives me his usual puppy-dog smile.

In that moment, it's simple enough to fake a sneeze, bring my hand up to my lips, and slip the hex powder under my tongue.

"Gesundheit," says Travis. He looks at me, melting.

The absolute, unambivalent love in his eyes is a thrill to behold. It makes me tingle and blush, and it seems only natural to take his hand.

And that's how it starts. Heads turn and mouths gape as we walk down the hall holding hands. Like a couple. Travis beams ear to ear, as if he's never been prouder.

The rumors start swirling like wildfire. Rachel crosses the hall to avoid meeting my eye, Kate flashes me a thumbs-up, and Megan and her mean-girl posse glower, as I knew they would. But I don't care what anyone thinks. Not even when Megan stalks up to me in the cafeteria and hisses, "I am taking you *down*, Big Bird," flipping my lunch tray into my lap in front of the whole room.

Kids whistle and hoot, yelling, "Catfight!" But I just look at Megan, serene.

Really? Really? I think, staring up at her. *That's the best you can do, a little barbecue sauce on my sundress?* Travis is already rushing my way with a paper towel.

The queen of monkeys looks furious but I'm not scared anymore.

Just wait until you see what comes back at you, Megan, I think. *You're going to be sorry you ever bullied or insulted anyone.*

I stay up way after midnight, poring over the spell book's revenge incantations. Eventually, I grind up powders and herbs for a potion that "Causes the Skin to Break Out in Hideous Spots." That ought to serve Megan right. I don't want to cause her lasting damage, but making her feel bad about how she looks will be sweet. Let *her* be the one with self-esteem issues.

Next I get to work on a hex powder called "To Turn Ally to Enemy," tipping it into a cafeteria saltshaker. Tomorrow that powder is going on Amber's and Sloane's French fries. Let Miss Popularity lose both of her sidekicks as well as her boyfriend, and see how it feels to turn into a pimple-faced nobody.

Gloating, I bend to blow out the last candle. In the sudden darkness, the wind blows my shutters wide open and I hear the tree branches tossing and creaking. The night sky is wild with an unearthly energy.

Good, I think. *Make this a power night.*

But taking revenge takes revenge on me: After I've finished mixing the potions, I can't fall asleep. My whole body is churned up and restless, and as I lie tossing and turning in bed, listening to the wind, I can't shake the sensation that my room is full of bad things, toads and spiders and rats scrabbling under the floorboards. When I finally sink into something that passes for sleep, it's riddled with nightmares.

The sky outside ripples with lightning, and the whole house seems to lurch and stretch, pushing up from the earth, getting taller and taller until it's a massive stone tower against the black sky.

A lightning bolt splits the roof open, making the whole room shake and hurling me out through my open window. Another body is falling beside mine, but I can't see his face. We fall down headfirst, tumbling through space into earthquakes that unzip the ground into chasms of fire.

I wake up in a cold sweat of terror. It's morning. Did any of that really happen, like the night I dreamed about Danielle's fire?

But no, the sky outside my window is a mild summer blue, with birds singing and dew on the grass. The only disaster is inside my head, which is throbbing with one of those awful spike headaches, the first one I've had in a long time. I pull on my clothes and carefully hide my potions inside my purse. I head downstairs, not acknowledging Dad, Matt, or Danielle. If that means skipping breakfast, I'll live.

I get into my car and shift into reverse. As I look in the rearview to back down the driveway, I let out a scream.

Rem is sitting in the backseat.

Chapter 12

"**WHAT ARE YOU DOING HERE?**" I SPLUTTER in shock. Did he break into my car? I turn in my seat to look toward the house, wondering if I should call out to Dad. Or call the police. I'm pretty sure no one heard my quick scream.

"I need to talk to you," Rem says steadily.

I glare at him. I'm not pleased that he looks just as gorgeous as ever. That's really not fair when I'm furious at him.

"Tell it to Kara," I snap. "Or didn't you know that I saw you two kissing?"

"Of course I knew. I *made* you see that."

I didn't expect that response. "What are you talking about?" I demand, more confused than ever.

"Not here," he says. "Someplace private. Let's go to the beach."

"Rem, I've got school!"

"You can't bring those revenge potions to school with you," he says, and the urgency in his voice stuns me as much as the fact that he knows about them.

"Are you spying on me?" I ask, shaking.

"Yes," he says bluntly. "Drive to the beach and I'll tell you why."

For a moment, I consider bursting out of the car, running back into the house. But upset as I am with him, I trust Rem to tell me the truth. And now I need answers.

The beach is not very far from my house, and we drive in uncomfortable silence. As soon as I park, on an empty lot wind-strewn with sand, Rem jumps out of the car. He heads into the dunes, and I realize that he's barefoot. It's not hard to see why — with every step my sneakers sink into deep sand. I bend down to take them off, tying their laces together with the knot Travis taught me and slinging them over my shoulder.

I follow Rem down to the tidal strip, edged with pop weed and fragments of clamshells. The sand here is hard-packed, with foamy waves rolling up to the edge. Rem keeps moving, anxiously seeking a place he deems private enough. What is he worried about, seagulls with spy-cams? There's a jogger a mile or so down the strand with his golden retriever, but other than that, the beach is completely deserted.

Finally, Rem stops at a weathered drift log, gesturing that I should sit. He sits down beside me, so close he can whisper. As if the roar of the breaking waves wouldn't drown out whatever he's planning to tell me.

"You know that our souls are connected," he murmurs, and right away my stomach jumps. I can't move, or speak. "Don't protest or say you don't feel it," he goes on. "I know you do. It's been there since the first time we met. That's how I know you've been practicing spells."

My eyebrows go up. "Are you saying you can read my mind?"

"Not all the time. Not when you're at school. But when you're doing magic, our energy's braided together. It has been for centuries."

This is starting to freak me out big-time. What is he saying? That he knows about my magic powers — believes in them? If it's all true, then why did he tell me at our swimming lesson that I was imagining things?

It wasn't the right time or place, his voice says in my head. Rem goes on in a spy-movie whisper. "We don't have much time," he says. "You haven't crossed all the way over yet. You can still stop."

"I don't know what you're talking about," I say with an edge. Stop what? Making the kind of potions I made last night?

"You know in your heart. There's no use pretending."

I stand up, frightened. "I've got trigonometry class." I start walking away, but Rem jumps up, grabbing my arm.

"I was supposed to bring you across. And they're furious I haven't done it yet."

My head is spinning. "Done what? Who are *they*?"

Rem's face grows serious. "All right, I'll make this quick. Twenty people were killed on charges of witchcraft in Salem in 1692."

I nod. I know this already. And Rem must know that I know it. My blood is roaring in my ears as I think of my ancestor Sarah Good. But she was proven innocent. Wasn't she?

"Every so often," Rem goes on, "one of their descendants is born with potential powers. Think of it as a rogue witch gene, like having red hair because someone way back in your ancestry had it." *Or being as pale as your mother when everyone else in your family is dark- and curly-haired*, I think, and nod.

"But," I begin, "if I was born with some witch gene for magical powers, wouldn't I already —"

"*Potential* powers," Rem corrects me. "Which usually start to appear at the age of sixteen."

Like my dreams and my headaches, I think. Rem is still talking.

"Sometimes that potential runs in a different direction and turns into artistic or musical talent; people call it a gift. But if it runs toward the rarer gift, actual magic, another witch is tapped to help them . . . cross over. Become a full witch."

Cross over. I open my mouth and manage to speak. "Like you were supposed to . . ." He nods again. "So you're . . . a *witch*?"

Rem turns his blue-and-green eyes on me. "Duh." There's a trace of a smile on his lips, and it brings out his dimples. Why does he have to be so irresistible?

I jerk away from him. "Don't make fun of me, Rem. You've got to admit this is hard to believe. And why didn't you tell me before?"

"Too risky. There's no place in Salem where someone's not watching and listening."

"What is it, witch Homeland Security?" I shiver, staring at him. It still seems unreal that we're talking about this.

"It isn't a joke. There are four kinds of witches in this world," Rem continues, "each tied to an element. I'm a water witch, through my grandmother's line. So are most of the witches in Salem, or anywhere else. There's a hand-ful of air witches, mostly half crazy."

I think of the elements as Dyami listed them when she did my tarot reading. *Water, air, earth, fire . . .*

"And earth witches?" I ask.

Rem shudders and lowers his voice. "One. Only one. But you, Abby? You're the rarest of all. There hasn't been a fire witch in Salem in three hundred years. And that's what you are."

A fire witch! Suddenly, things seem to fall into place. The candles bursting into flame, Danielle's house, my dreams of fire, my fear of water . . .

And what Rem said to me that day of our swim lesson: *"I can see the fire in your eyes."*

I look at Rem now, and I know in my heart that he's telling the truth.

His voice picks up urgency, as if he's afraid he won't have time to finish. "There must be a witch of each element to complete the circle," he's saying, "so they can bring Salem to justice. The air witch is losing her grip on this lifetime, and the earth witch is on the move. He's looking for us right this minute. The ocean is drowning us out, but he knows we're nearby. I can feel him searching. Can't you?"

Now I'm really spooked. I do feel a presence, as clammy and deep as an underground cave. I shiver, and Rem pulls me close. I bury my face in his neck. His skin smells like saltwater taffy, briny and sweet. I can feel his heart beating against mine, the strong, reassuring warmth of his body, and it feels so perfectly right that I raise my face to his. *Kiss me*, I think. *Kiss me now.*

But Rem pulls away. Again.

"Why do you *do* that?" I blurt out. "Because of Kara?"

He shakes his head. "Because of you."

"I don't understand."

"A witch's kiss is a dangerous thing, Abby. It transfers and magnifies powers. When one of us kisses a human, it can turn them into a witch."

"But I'm already a witch."

"No, you're not. You're just a beginner. The powers you've already harnessed are nothing compared to what you have inside you. If I give you the witch's kiss, there'll be no turning back. For either of us."

"But you were kissing Kara. I saw you."

Rem sighs. "Kara is a fourth-degree water witch. Her powers aren't strong — never will be. But you've got the strong bloodlines, and fire is the rarest of all the magical elements, the one that's been missing from Salem for centuries. That's why they want you to cross over *now.*"

I study his face. "You keep saying 'they.' Not 'we.'"

"I'm only half witch. And my human half wants to protect you."

My eyes open wide as I put it together. "That's why you keep turning away."

Rem nods, looking miserable. "I was supposed to make you fall in love with me, so I could give you the witch's kiss and seal the deal."

I bristle. "Supposed to? What am I, your *homework*?"

"That was the plan. But . . ."

But what, Rem? This better be good.

I hear the roar of the ocean behind us as he lifts his eyes, looking right into mine. "But my human half fell in love with you first."

Oh. Wow, that *is* good. My heart starts to flutter.

And then I remember. "But what about Kara?"

Rem sighs again. "That was such a mistake. I thought I could make you jealous and drive you away from me. But if you keep casting spells on your own, you'll still be in danger. They want you to come fully into your powers, so you can bring fire to the circle and gather the storm." He takes my hand, imploring. "You're still much more human than witch, but every time you cast a spell, your powers get stronger. Look at yourself, Abby. Even your eyes are changing. That's the sign. Promise me you'll stop doing magic."

"How can I promise? I don't even know how it works! Sometimes I just think really hard and things happen. Like moving that traffic cone."

"That's how you got onto our radar. Esperanza spotted you." With a gasp, I remember the RMV tester with the long dark hair, the way that she stared at me after the cone moved. "And that led you straight to the Double Double Café."

"To meet you."

Rem nods, looking guilty.

"Except nobody led me," I challenge him. "I was the one who decided to go to Salem, and I was the one who picked out the café."

"Magic always makes you think you're the one making the choices. Does Travis know he's being led?"

I wince. Rem knows about Travis? Now it's my turn to look guilty.

Of course I know, he says inside my head. *Our souls are connected, remember?*

"Then why can't we —"

Rem stops me short. "If we kiss, you'll become a full witch. Forever."

"You said a witch's kiss *transfers* power. Couldn't I make you human forever?"

"The stronger energy always replaces the weaker. That's why the earth witch wants me to finish the task."

A harsh gust of wind shears sand off the dunes. It swirls in an angry cloud, stinging our faces, and I feel a sudden deep dread in the pit of my stomach.

"He's found us," Rem whispers. "Go back to your school, to your human boy. Steer clear of Salem and don't practice magic. I've got to go."

"But . . ." There are so many ways I could finish that sentence. I land on one of the weakest. "How will you get back home?"

Rem points to the edge of the dunes, where he's hidden his kayak. "I'll be fine, Abby. You can still choose to stay human. It isn't too late" is the last thing he says.

I *am* late for school, though. Incredibly late. I've missed trig altogether, and I slink into Ms. Baptiste's classroom midway through a pop quiz. There's so much swirling around in my mind that I can't focus at all. It occurs to me that I'm already keeping my promise to Rem: In place of the magic that's been guiding my fingers to circle the right answer every time is a totally human confusion, as real as the sand in my sneakers.

"All right, turn them in, people. No extra time!" Ms.

Baptiste calls. Students grumble and pass their papers down the rows to Samson Hobby, who's been put in the front row for attitude issues, giving us all a prime view of his stubbly new Mohawk.

I carry my test up to Ms. Baptiste's desk instead. "I missed most of class," I say. "Can I take the rest of the quiz during my study hall?"

She frowns, fixing me with a steely-eyed stare. "If I can trust you not to consult any books in between," she says. "How's that extra-credit research project on Salem coming?"

Wrong question. I kind of forgot about that, even though Salem itself has been on my mind nonstop. "I'll get it to you really soon," I say, blushing. "I've just had a lot . . . going on."

She leans back and studies me over the top of her glasses. "I'm sure you have," she says drily.

I'm not sure what she means by that. I never think teachers pay much attention to the gossip mill that's so all-consuming in Ipswich High School. But Megan's smear campaign against me would be hard to miss.

She's been calling out "Hey, Big Bird!" and "What's up, Scabigail?" every time I pass her and her friends in the hall. She's even started a Facebook page called the "Pick at a Scabigail Group," which makes my stomach hurt every time I see it pop up on-screen with more Likes. I've stopped going online, just so I won't have to deal with all the mean comments. It seems a steep price for getting Travis to fall for me. Especially if my soul is connected to Rem's.

As I walk out of Ms. Baptiste's class and down the hall, I see people smirking and whispering to each other, or turning their heads from their lockers to stare as I pass. I do my best to ignore them and hold my head high, even when I overhear a boy in a track jacket say to his friend, "Who, *her*? Is he blind?"

To make matters worse, Rachel is still barely speaking to me. We don't meet up before and after school, text, or talk like we used to. The only person who's still in my corner is Kate. She says Megan is blacklisting me, like her grandfather was blacklisted in the 1950s, during what she calls "the Communist witch hunt." I don't tell Kate how right on the money she is.

And Travis, of course, is also in my corner, loyal and true. He keeps asking me to bake something for him. I'd be happy to whip up a batch of non-magical cupcakes, but the kitchen's no longer my own.

It's Danielle's.

She's now moved in with a vengeance. Dad and I used to split grocery shopping and laundry chores, but she's taken over those duties full-force. It's a relief not to have to do all the grunt work, but every time I open the fridge to a new brand of orange juice or find her socks mixed in with mine in the dryer, I feel invaded.

It doesn't help that, in spite of the stresses of dealing with insurance claims and repairmen, she's been unfailingly pleasant to me. Nice in a sort of slick way that has to do both with her hostess profession *and* with her seeing me as a problem to solve — New Mate's Hostile Daughter — instead of a specific person with likes and dislikes and her own set of issues. Issues Danielle couldn't even begin to imagine.

And, of course, Matt thinks she's great. He's a nine-year-old boy; you can win him over with chocolate-chip pancakes and Tater Tots. Easy as pie. Which Danielle also bakes, in the oven that used to be my private domain. Dad is happier than he's been in years, which I am glad to see, but also makes me — again — the odd one out in my family. And it doesn't escape me that Danielle is living in our house because of the fire I started.

Any lingering doubts I had about whether I really have magical powers were put to rest by Rem telling me I'm a fire witch. *The* fire witch, apparently, the one the witches of Salem have been seeking for hundreds of years.

I didn't ask for any of this, but it seems that the hand I got dealt in this life was a literal burning rage. If the thoughts in my head can start fires, I better watch out what I think of Danielle. Of everyone.

All day Friday I waver back and forth — should I go to Salem tomorrow morning, or not? I sit in my classes, mulling it over. It's really not fair to Dyami if I quit my job with no notice, especially now that it's getting into prime summer season. And what would I even tell her? "I'm sorry, I'm scared I'll turn into a witch forever if I come to work" sounds ridiculous by any standards. Besides, I'm still paying my cousin Roberto. I don't want to give up my car.

In the end, I decide that I will go to work, but I'll honor Rem's wishes and steer clear of him. No more double caramel mochas for breakfast; I'll have to buy my coffee at Dunkin' Donuts like everyone else.

Well, at least I won't have to see Kara.

The irony hits me between the eyes. Rem can kiss Kara; she's already crossed over. But he won't ever kiss me.

And why? Because his human side wants to protect me. I feel a swell of joy mixed with sorrow at the realization. He can't kiss me, because he's in love with me.

Chapter 13

I WAKE UP BEFORE THE ALARM CLOCK ON Saturday morning. No nightmares at all, and no headache either, which seems like some kind of a miracle. If they were the first sign of my witchy powers, maybe they'll go away if I keep my promise to Rem and stop practicing magic.

It's something to hope for, at least.

I brush my teeth, pull my clothes on, and head down the stairs to the kitchen. Dad is already wearing his soccer coach uniform, and Danielle's fixing him an egg sandwich with bacon and cheddar.

"Good morning, Abby." She smiles, putting the sandwich onto a plate and reaching for a bottle of ketchup. "Would you like me to make you one?"

I shake my head. "I can't face that much food when I first wake up. Thanks for the offer, though."

Dad looks up from his coffee, grateful that I'm being nice to his girlfriend for a change. "How about some juice?" Danielle offers. She opens the fridge. "You can take it to go, if you'd rather."

"I don't need to —" I stop in mid-sentence. Why not just say yes? It'll make her so happy. "Sure."

Danielle smiles, pouring orange juice into a travel cup. "Here you go."

"Thanks," I say, taking it from her and waving at Dad. "I'll see you both later."

I can't help it. That "both" makes me wince.

I don't touch the orange juice. My stomach's unsettled, and my whole body feels heavy and sluggish, even though the weather could not be more perfect. It's as if the morning is posing for June on a calendar. I roll down my front window as I drive along the familiar roads with the radio cranked to my favorite oldies station. The air's mild and sweet, with a whiff of wild roses and salt air. When I get to Beverly Bay, I see more sailboats and windsurfers out on the water than ever before.

Usually this is where I would take a deep breath, anticipating the surge of excitement that bubbles inside me whenever I cross the bridge over this span of water. But my spirits don't lift in the usual way. It's not hard to figure out why: A big part of the reason my heart swelled every time was the prospect of seeing Rem.

Not only do I know full well that he's not going to let himself bump into me accidentally-on-purpose, I'm also freaked out by the things he's told me about Salem. Behind all the quaintness, touristy witch-kitsch, and Halloween trappings lurks a secret society of actual witches, including an earth witch who apparently scares even Rem. And these unknown witches seem to be holding the reins on a lot of decisions I thought were my own, moving me like a puppet and listening in on my innermost thoughts. Just the idea of it makes my skin crawl.

So when that same perfect parking spot that's been open for me twice before, right in front of Double Double, turns out to be empty again, it doesn't feel like a stroke of good luck — it gives me the cold creeps. I drive right past it deliberately and leave my car parked in front of an abandoned dry cleaners on a back street several blocks away.

I walk back toward Dyami's store via a series of residential side streets, where the everyday sights of little kids bombing around on brightly colored tricycles and a middle-aged woman unloading her grocery cart help me to calm down a little.

This town isn't all sinister. There are Laundromats and gas stations, college students and hardware store clerks, old men wearing windbreakers and Velcro sneakers out walking their dogs, just like anyplace else. As a fringe benefit, parking on the back street means that I'll be approaching Spiral Visions from the opposite direction, so I won't have to walk past the Double Double Café. I don't want to know if Rem is at work today, and I certainly don't want to cross paths with Kara.

"Something is making you sad today," says Dyami after I arrive. She passes her hand just above my head "to calm the crown chakra." For a moment, I wonder if she's a witch, too. Anyone could be — who would have guessed there were witches who give drivers' tests? And Rem said there were many of them, descendants of the old witches, here in Salem. But Dyami's eyes are a solid, comforting brown — no streak of gold or silver. Her gift isn't magic, but pure intuition.

She's right, I am feeling a little bit sad. Especially when I head out for my lunch break and have to avoid all the places I've eaten with Rem — Ugly Gus, Benny's Pizza, the Polish place that makes those delicious pierogi. There are memories everywhere, but I do what Rem told me to do and steer clear of any place where I might come across him. Or miss him too much.

To continue my good-girl streak, on my way home from work, I stop at one of the town's several witch-themed museums. I promised Ms. Baptiste I would do more research, and I want to find out not just about my own ancestors but the rest of the people involved with the trials. Especially now, given what I know. If the living witches who haunt Salem now — the ones plotting some kind of revenge scheme they want me to join — are descended from the accused who were sent to their deaths in 1692, I need to find out all I can about who those people were.

As I wait in a long line of tourists, I study the eyes of the old woman taking admissions, but they're both the same shade of patrician blue. I feel a small wave of relief, pay her the fee, and go inside.

The exhibit shows large dioramas depicting the Salem witch trials. And each diorama gets more and more under my skin. It was hard enough reading about these dark times, but seeing the images in three dimensions is so much more visceral. The life-size wax museum figures are like scenes from my nightmares — the afflicted girls in their dark dresses and white aprons writhing in fits, dark-robed men in Puritan hats, fingers pointing. When I see the likeness of Reverend Nicholas Noyes, the man Sarah Good cursed from the gallows, it's all I can do to keep breathing.

He's not real, I remind myself. *He's molded wax with glass eyes and horsehair.*

Then I come upon a diorama showing Sarah Good in her prison cell. It tears at my heart. Gaunt and pale, her pregnancy poorly hidden beneath threadbare garments, my ancestor looks feral, defiant. But it's little Dorcas who haunts me the most. When I turn my eyes to the smallest wax figure, I can feel her inconsolable cries echoing somewhere deep inside my bones. My own eyes sting with tears. Are they for that long-ago girl who lost her mother so young . . . or for myself? .

I force myself to move on to the next diorama. A lot of the names are familiar from my research reading, but some things are brand-new to me. One thing I didn't know is that only nineteen of those who died were sentenced to hang. At least four died in prison before being convicted. The last, a tough-minded farmer named Giles Corey, adamantly refused to testify. He was pressed to death beneath heavy stones, with more and more weight added until his bones cracked and his heart burst. I can't imagine how painful his death must have been, and I wonder if his tortured spirit is one of the ones that's come back to wreak vengeance on Salem.

Could his descendant, in fact, be the earth witch Rem warned me about? But there's no mention of the four elements on any of the placards. The history Rem told me doesn't exist in the official versions; it's under-ground lore.

I leave the museum shaken, wondering how much goes on in the world that's not written in history books, that we can't understand. We're told as children that witches aren't real — and neither are vampires, werewolves, or ghosts. But if that's the case, why have their stories been passed down for centuries?

And of course now I know why. Because sometimes they're true. It's as if there's another world lurking just under-neath ours, and sometimes, not often, the veil between worlds gets a little bit threadbare and something slips through it.

This is on my mind as I'm driving back home, espe-cially when I take a wrong turn on the highway I've driven on many times, and wind up right outside Great-aunt Gail's nursing home.

I'm about to back up and get back on my route when I'm seized with the impulse to go in and visit her. It doesn't make any sense, but it's almost as if I've been hypnotized. Without any conscious decision to do it, I find myself parking my car, heading into the Muzak-filled lobby, and signing my name in the guest book at the front desk.

When the elevator lets me out onto the grim second floor, the first person I see is the West Indian nurse with the dreadlocks. Her nails are bright coral today.

"You seeing Miz Solart, darlin'?" she asks. "I'm sorry to tell you, but she had a partial stroke. Hasn't spoken a word since the last time you came."

She makes this sound as if this is a blessing. I bet the whole nursing staff is relieved that Great-aunt Gail's no longer spitting out crazy words and curses. It does make it seem even more pointless to go to her room, but again, it's as if something is pulling me forward.

Fighting the uneasy dread in the pit of my stomach, I walk down the olive-drab hallway, lined with inert older people in wheelchairs. One man's toothless mouth is wide open, his eyes blank and staring. Edging away from his side of the hall, I nearly trip over the bony feet of the woman across from him. "Sorry," I say, and she grunts out a sound without consonants.

The door to Gail's room is propped open, and I leave it that way as I slip inside. Her shrunken form lies underneath a blue sheet. She is staring up at the ceiling with unseeing eyes, and my first thought is that she might have died. Is this what a stroke looks like?

As I take a few tentative steps toward her bed, a stray gust of wind blows the door shut.

The sound of its slam makes me startle — and so does the realization that her window's latched closed; there's no way the wind could have blown through it. A split second later, the top of her hospital bed's rising up at an angle. She's staring right at me, the dark streak across her left eye unmistakable.

"Aunt Gail?" I say, fearful.

"Take up your place in the circle," she rasps. "Time is short."

My heart starts to pound. "I don't know what you mean —"

"Of course you do, Dorcas. You're one of us."

"Why are you calling me Dorcas?" I stammer.

"I'm too old to keep the names straight. You're part of her family. The husk doesn't matter." She gives me a stern look. "What matters is claiming your powers before the full moon. That Indian boy's filled your head up with nonsense."

My heart clutches.

She knows about Rem?

Gail answers as if she had heard my thoughts, her voice gaining power. "That boy is a tadpole, too weak to conduct you, but you have a fiery furnace inside. In just these few weeks, you've learned more of the craft than most do in two lifetimes. That's why we sent you the spell book. We knew it would tempt you to practice. When you finish crossing, you will be a force to be reckoned with."

"What if I don't want to?" I tell her, defiant.

"It's all preordained," she says, fixing her darkening eye on me. "Earth's on his way, and he knows who you are. You can't escape your fate."

There's a rap at the door, and I swivel around as the dreadlocked nurse swings it open. She looks at my face.

"Are you okay, darlin'? You look like you just saw a ghost."

I glance back at Great-aunt Gail. She's lying flat on her back, as unresponsive and rigid as she was when I entered. Her eyes are a blank, milky blue.

"Did you hear her talking?" I ask the nurse, trying to swallow my panic. "Was that why you knocked?"

"I didn't hear nothing," she tells me, rolling a tray toward the hospital bed. "Just came in to check on her vitals. Why, was she trying to say something to you?"

I nod. She was saying something, all right. Something I would never have believed before everything in my life changed.

But now I believe every word.

Chapter 14

THERE'S A WEIRD STILLNESS HOVERING OVER
Salem the following morning. Flags and banners hang limp on their poles, and the warm air seems sweaty; there might be a summer storm brewing. Tourists come into the store fanning themselves with brochures, exclaiming gratefully over our air-conditioning. Most people use the word "muggy," but Dyami has a different explanation.

"It's hanging season," she tells me. "The energy always gets strange on the anniversaries."

"Anniversaries of —"

"The hangings on Gallows Hill," she says.

Somehow when I read the list of names at the museum, I didn't notice the dates of the hangings. Dyami tells me they started in June and went on through September. "Even all these years later, the atmosphere's charged. You can sense an ionic disturbance. Especially during the full moon."

A shiver runs through me as I remember Gail's words. *What matters is claiming your powers before the full moon.*

"When is the next full moon?" I ask, and Dyami smiles.

"It's on June twenty-first. That ought to be quite the power night. Summer solstice, midsummer night, and a full moon."

Add two more to that list. Some kind of witches' circle I'm supposed to take part in on Gallows Hill. And Ipswich High prom night.

As I'm leaving work at the end of the day, I notice the Double Double Café awning is moving. My pulse quickens as I realize Rem must be cranking it up for the night. I can't resist going to see him. He must know I've been good and haven't been casting any spells. How much could it hurt to say hi?

But when I turn the corner, it isn't Rem turning the crank. Kara shoots me a knowing look and says, "Rem isn't here today. He hasn't shown up all weekend."

My cheeks flush as I nod, disappointed. But as I head back to my car, a sudden fear grips me. *Gail knew Rem was trying to keep me from crossing over.* What if the rest of the witches did, too? Might they have done something to punish him?

I have to find him. Even if it means breaking my

promise. If anything's happened to Rem, I'll be devastated. Especially if it's because of me.

The marina seems ten times as far as the last time I went, and I know it's because I'm so anxious. My heart's hammering inside my chest as I rush through the gate, past the dry-dock racks, down to the dock . . .

And the floating bridge.

As soon as I put one foot onto it, it bobs up and down. How am I going to do this? I'm still clinging tight to the piling alongside the dock, but to get to the tugboat, I'll have to let go. I close my eyes — just for a moment — and picture Rem standing in chest-high water, holding me up with his arms. Like a magician's assistant, he told me. *I've got you.*

And then he let go. So that I could do it by myself.

I open my eyes. I *can* do it by myself. I can let go of this piling and put one foot forward, and then the next. There, see? I'm doing it.

One foot. Then another.

The bridge bobs and wobbles with every step, and I just keep edging my way forward. I grit my teeth, trying to concentrate.

Suddenly, for just a split second, I see a dark figure reflected in the rippling water: a tall man dressed in black. I look up, but there's nobody there. The reflection is gone, too. A shiver runs through me, so cold I get goose bumps.

What *was* that, a vision? Am I having nightmares in daylight?

I can't think about it right now. One foot. Then another. And finally I'm there. When my hand catches hold of the tugboat's rail, I'm so grateful I think I will faint.

I rap on a porthole. "Rem?" I call. "Rem? Are you there?"

There's no answer.

Where is he? My heart pounds with fear for his safety. And mine. *Tell me I don't have to get right back onto that bridge.*

Then I feel the boat creak and rock. Someone's moving inside; I hear footsteps approaching. Is it Rem, or the sinister man whose reflection I saw in the water?

I hold my breath as the door of the cabin swings open. Rem stands on the threshold, sun-kissed and tousle-haired, smiling at me as if nothing is wrong, or has ever been wrong. I've never been gladder to see anyone in my life. Not even the knowledge that I broke my promise by coming here spoils the moment. His smile floods my whole body with joy. How could I stay away?

"Abby!" he says, grinning wider. "You conquered the bridge!"

"I was so worried about you," I tell him. "Can I come inside?"

"I've got an even better idea," says Rem. His green-

and-blue eyes catch the pinpoints of light off the water. Maybe that's what makes them glitter more sharply than usual. I'm reminded, for just the breath of a second, of the shiny glass eyes in the witch wax museum. "Let's go for a walk. There's a place I've been meaning to show you."

Rem takes me to a wooded park on the outskirts of town. There's a flat stretch of grass with a softball field, and behind it a rise toward a dark fringe of trees. A narrow footpath leads up to the top of the hill, and as we start walking up it, Rem pulls me away from its edge. "Watch out for those burdocks. They'll stick to your clothes."

We climb up in single file. He leads the way and I follow him, wondering why such a small incline makes my breath come in pants. I'm more out of shape than I realized; I should sign up for one of those charity runs Travis does.

I step over a root and feel a sudden sensation of heaviness inside my bones. One of those ice-pick headaches stabs into the base of my skull, and I realize that I'm gasping for breath — not just because the climb's gotten steeper, but as if something invisible's tightened around my neck, choking me like a noose.

Could this be Gallows Hill? Why would Rem want to take me to this evil place? I don't understand. And I feel weaker with every step, as if I can't breathe.

"Rem?" I pant. "Can we stop for a minute?"

"Of course," he says, turning to face me. The off-color streak in his left eye seems to pulsate as he puts his hands on my upper arms. His touch sends a tingle right through me.

"I couldn't stop thinking about you," he says, his voice getting husky. "I missed you like crazy."

I drink in his words — they're exactly what I've longed to hear — but something is off, and it's not just my headache. Rem's looking at me like a ravenous predator, ready to strike. Before I can speak, he's pulling me closer, his strong arms wrapping around my back. His lips burrow into the side of my neck, working their way toward my mouth.

"What are you doing?" I gasp. "You told me we couldn't —"

"Forget what I told you," he says. "You know we both want the same thing."

No, we don't. Not like this.

I struggle to free myself. He's much stronger than I am — superhumanly strong — but I feel an angry heat rising in my veins, like lava. I wrench myself free.

"Stop it," I hiss, and he staggers back, pressing one hand to his mouth as if he's been burned.

I turn away from him and nearly bump into a man who seems to appear as if out of thin air. I gasp as I realize he is the dark figure I saw before. He's gaunt and lank-haired, in a battered black leather trench coat. His features are ancient and sinister, with a wide, fleshy mouth, hollow cheeks, and a long crooked nose. But what draws me at once are his eyes, heavy-lidded, hypnotic, and dark as twin ink spots.

"Fiery," he says with a satisfied leer. "Just as you should be." His voice is as deep as a mine shaft.

He twists his gaze toward the sky, where a rust-colored crescent moon has just cleared the trees at the top of the hill. When he looks back at me, the top quadrant of his left eye glows with the same rusty red.

"The full moon is coming," he intones. "And with or without the kiss, you'll take your place in the circle, right here on Gallows Hill. The cycle will finally be finished. You can't turn your back on a gathering storm."

I wake up on the tugboat. I'm flat on my back on a bench, and Rem's kneeling beside me, holding a wet cloth to my forehead.

"What — what happened?" I stammer.

"You fainted," he tells me.

I blink, and the back of my skull throbs with pain as I try to remember.

"We were someplace else. On a hill. And you tried to kiss —"

Rem cuts me off sharply. "I didn't do anything. You had a dream. A hallucination."

I shake my head, insistent. "There was a man in a black coat. He said — he said something about Gallows Hill. . . ."

Rem frowns. "You hit your head," he says without meeting my eye.

I sit up, swinging my legs to the ground. As my hand brushes against my skirt, something snags at my skin. I look down and see spiky burdock seeds stuck to the fabric. My pulse starts to race.

"Rem, you were there. You *did* try to give me the witch's kiss. Why are you lying to me?" My voice sounds hysterical, even to me, but it freaks me out that he's not telling the truth.

Or is he? If we really were on Gallows Hill, how did we get back to the tugboat?

Wait, don't tell me. Magic. We probably flew on a broomstick.

This whole thing is scaring me out of my wits. My head is still pounding. I feel like I'm running a fever.

Fiery. Just as you should be.

The sinister man's words sear across my brain. I remember him telling me I'll take my place in the circle, that the cycle will finally be finished. Is this really some kind of three-hundred-year-old revenge fantasy? And whose side is Rem on?

I can't tell anymore. I don't know who he is. I can't trust my own soul mate.

"I've got to get home," I say, reeling up off the bench.

"What are you doing?" Rem says, his voice sharp with worry. "You just hit your head. What if you have a concussion?"

"My dad will be worried. I've got to get home," I repeat. I climb over the rail and step down to the wobbly bridge. Heart in my throat, I start scuttling along it, moving too fast. When Rem jumps down after me, I lose my balance — and plunge headlong into the water.

It's freezing cold, and I can't stifle a scream. In an instant, my mouth and nose fill up with water. The weight of my soaking skirt pulls me down as I thrash in terror. My eyes are wide open, and I see a dark fringe of trees overhead as I sink. It's the living image of my drowning nightmare.

Except that Rem jumps off the dock, slings his arm around me like a lifeguard, and swims with strong strokes toward the shore. He hauls me up onto the sand, where I sputter and cough, spitting out salt water.

Rem leans over me, panting and soaked to the skin. Our faces are inches apart. Is he going to give me mouth-to-mouth resuscitation?

I want him to kiss me, right now, more than I've ever wanted anything. A sense of surrender flows through my whole body. I don't care what happens; we should be kissing. I reach my hands up to his neck, arching my mouth toward his. But Rem draws back, his eyes flashing.

"Abby, that man is the earth witch! He's trying to drag you into the circle through me, can't you see that? He can make me do things I don't want to do. I've been pushing against him with all of my strength. And you're playing right into his hands!"

My teeth start to chatter, from fear or the cold, or more likely both. "I'm scared," I say. I cling to Rem's arm, but he pulls away, backing up fast.

"Stay away from me, Abby. I already told you that. I can't protect you. I'm the one you need protection from." He dives into the water and swims away, leaving me soaked, miserable, and completely alone.

Chapter 15

I FEEL LIKE A DROWNED RAT. I'VE CRANKED up my car's heater, but it hasn't kicked in yet. I'm drenched to the skin and my teeth are rattling away like maracas. I feel like I'll never get warm again. I can't forgive Rem for abandoning me. If the earth witch is as all-powerful as Rem says, how could Rem swim off and leave me alone on the beach? Anything could have happened.

My head throbs, and I vow that I'll never go near Rem again. If that's what he wanted, he's got it. I'm sick of his endless excuses and cryptic pronouncements. I don't care how alluring he is. That's the last time I'm going to let him pull me close and then push me away.

As soon as I've crossed the bridge back to Beverly, my spike headache lifts, and with it my dread. This is the real world all around me, a suburban sprawl full of cheap Chinese restaurants and diners and twenty-four-hour Rite-Aids.

There aren't evil earth witches who look like Keith Richards with blood in their eyes, and I'm not the fire witch of Salem who's come back to "take my place in the circle" or "complete the cycle" or whatever mumbo jumbo is filling my head. I've seen too many fantasy movies — if I'm having some kind of schizophrenic breakdown, the voices inside my head sound like Gandalf the Grey.

Enough of this nonsense. I'm nobody's witch. I'm just a teenage girl in soaking-wet clothes, mad at a boy who left her in the lurch, on her way home from work.

The next morning Travis parks right next to me in the school parking lot. When he sees me, he turns on the full warmth of his puppy-dog smile. "Hi, Abby," he says, pushing his cool vintage sunglasses on top of his head. "You look nice today."

What a relief! No tormented brooding or mixed messages. A friendly, cute boy with perfect blue eyes who thinks I look *nice*.

"Thanks," I say, feeling a welcome blush rise to my cheeks. On impulse I ask him if I can try on his sunglasses.

"Of course," he says, taking them off and handing them to me. I slip them on, realizing the tortoiseshell frames are still warm. It feels like being kissed on the backs of both ears.

Travis and I walk into school side by side. Jaws drop and heads swivel from lockers at the sight of me wearing his signature sunglasses.

Go ahead, somebody tell the queen of monkeys, I think as we stroll past a prom poster. *Bring it on.*

No sooner said than done. As I'm heading for my Spanish IV class, Megan turns the corner, flanked by Sloane and Amber. (Why are they *always* together? Are they taking all the same classes?)

"Give them to me," Megan says, holding her palm out. I can see the white moons of her French manicure.

"Give what to you, Megan?" I ask sweetly.

"Travis's glasses. I know you've got them."

I reach into my purse and take out the sunglasses. "You mean these?"

She grabs for them, but I lift them above my head, out of her reach. Even in heels, she's much shorter than me.

"I will return them when the person who gave them to me tells me he wants them back," I say coolly. "Got to go. I've got Español."

I never imagined that I could behave like this, but if Rem doesn't want to go near me and Travis does, why should I let his forever-mean girlfriend stand in my way?

Señora Ortiz has come to the door of her classroom, and stands waiting to close it behind me. As I stride past her, I slip on Travis's sunglasses, turning back to wave over my shoulder at Megan. *"Hasta la vista, tonta!"*

Señora Ortiz frowns, closing the door behind me. Kate Reeder is grinning especially wide, and Makayla Graf, the multi-pierced, turquoise-haired art student, slaps me five as I walk past her desk, saying, "You go, girl. Way to get in her *face!*"

My elation is short-lived. At dinner that night, Danielle seems especially bubbly. As she passes a platter of stuffed clams — I've got to admit it, she is a halfway decent cook — I notice she's wearing a new silver ring on her right hand. The design — a Celtic claddagh ring, with two hands holding a crowned heart — is one we stock at Spiral Visions. So I know what it symbolizes: a promise of love.

I stare at her fingers, not taking the platter. "Is that new?"

Danielle nods happily. "Your dad gave it to me last night. Isn't it beautiful?"

Matt stops chewing. "Are you guys gonna get married?"

Danielle and Dad both look a little embarrassed. "Not this week," Dad says lightly. He takes her hand. "It's our two-month anniversary. I wanted to give Danielle something special."

I stare at Dad. *I'm sorry, you lost me at "Not this week."*

That was so not what I wanted to hear. How about "Not ever"? How about "You kids are my family. She's an extracurricular activity"?

It's been hard enough to adjust to Danielle staying at our house while she gets new windows and carpets installed. I'm not ready to think about her moving in for the rest of our lives. Taking Mom's place at the table, taking over my kitchen, hogging my father's attention, spoiling Matt rotten, and making me feel like even more of an outsider.

It isn't her fault, I tell myself. She's been trying her best to be friendly to me. I just don't want her here. Which makes me feel extra guilty, since I'm the reason she had to move in.

"It's a beautiful ring," I say woodenly. Danielle gives me a warm smile, but Dad knows me well enough to realize that my heart isn't in it. He studies me in a concerned way. What does he expect from me, cartwheels? He's just lucky that I haven't set his girlfriend's hair on fire.

Yet.

I shake my head, as if to banish the very thought. Even the most random things that pop into my head seem dangerous now.

Danielle is holding the platter in front of me so I can serve myself. I scoop some clams onto my plate, but the sight of that claddagh ring torpedoes my appetite. I have no idea how I'm going to choke down this dinner. As I watch Danielle and Dad and Matt smiling and laughing and passing the peas, I feel as if I've got a hole in my heart that nobody can fill.

My cell phone goes off in my pocket. Dad frowns. "No texting at dinner. House rule." But Danielle puts her hand over his, her look implying he might want to cut me some slack. I'm struck by her tact. She didn't challenge his parental authority, but she still managed to let me know she would be on my side.

"All right, see who it is," Dad says grudgingly. "But answer it later."

I take out the phone and look at the screen. It's from Travis.

wd u like 2 go 4 a drive 2nite?

Why, yes, in fact. I would like that a lot.

"I'm so glad you were free." Travis glances at me from the wheel of his convertible. "I want to show you one of my favorite views on the planet."

"It's already a beautiful view," I respond, looking out at the grassy dunes we're driving past. The long, early summer dusk has painted the sky a deep lavender-gray, and the wind rushing over us smells of the sea.

"Wait," Travis tells me. "It's just up this next hill." As the car starts to climb, he glances over at me again. I enjoy his eyes on me, but I wish he'd focus on the steep road. "It works best if you close your eyes, so you won't get any hints."

"All right," I say, smiling. I let my eyes close and lean back into the leather upholstery. I can hear the car's engine, the rumble of tires over gravel. "Tell me when."

"Soon," Travis says, and I feel the car downshift and roll to a stop. He cuts the ignition, and I hear his door open.

"What are you —"

"Coming to get you. Keep your eyes closed." His footsteps circle around the car, and I hear him open the door on my side. He gives me his hand and helps me get out of the seat. Then he puts his arm over my shoulder. The warmth and weight of it makes me a little bit breathless, and I lean into him as he leads me a few steps away from the car. I can feel a smile spreading across my face. *Take that, Rem.*

"I feel like I'm pinning a tail on the donkey," I tell him.

"It's worth it," says Travis. We stop in place. "Okay, now."

I open my eyes, and a gasp escapes me. We're standing on top of a bluff overlooking Ipswich Bay. The pale curves of beaches and sandbars stretch out below, and the low-slung half-moon casts a shimmering ribbon of light across the dark water.

"It's beautiful, isn't it?" Travis says, and I nod. If I squint, I can make out the red and green running lights of a couple of Gloucester-bound trawlers, and the bright, steady pulse of a lighthouse.

"Which lighthouse is that?" I ask.

"The Annisquam Light," he says. "One of my favorites."

I look at him, surprised. How many seventeen-year-old guys have a favorite lighthouse? Travis shrugs. "I did a Gloucester road race that passes two other old lighthouses, and got this idea to visit them all. There are twelve on the North Shore."

"That's cool," I say. "There's one outside Salem," I add, my voice catching on the name of the town.

"Two," he says. "Derby Wharf and Fort Pickering." He shrugs again, grinning. "I know, kind of nerdy. I've always liked lighthouses. The way that they're just always *there*, you know? Keeping the light on."

A little like you, I think. Travis still has his arm around me, and the strong, solid warmth of it over my shoulder feels natural.

"Abby?" he says. "Can I ask you something?"

I turn to face him, feeling a flutter of nervous excitement. "Of course," I say.

"Would you go to the prom with me?"

A rush of emotions sweeps through me. There's the thrill of surprise. There's a sense of victory when I think of

Rem, and a nagging sense of defeat when I think of the spells I cast to get Trevor to this place. And then —

"But what about Megan?" I blurt, and then back up quickly when Travis's face tightens. "Yes, Travis. I'd love to go to prom with you. I just meant —"

"I know," he says. "But I broke up with Megan. I can't think of anybody but you. I just . . ." He looks at me, his eyes flooded with feeling. If I got this abiding love out of a bottle, I really did well. It feels totally real. "Did you just say you'd love to?" he asks, grinning.

I nod. And then Travis does something that makes my heart soar. He leans down and kisses me. Right on the lips.

They say your first kiss is the one you'll never forget, and I can see why. It's not just the wonderful new sensation, or the sweetness of Travis's lips. It's the fact that we *can* kiss. It won't turn me into a witch. If anything, it makes me feel even more human. I'm not some half-magical freak. I'm a happy sixteen-year-old who's being kissed by her prom date.

The news travels through Ipswich High like a run through a stocking. Wherever I go, people whisper and point at me. Megan is playing the tragic victim, with puddles of eyeliner underneath her red-rimmed eyes. But Amber and especially Sloane have turned into a pair of attack dogs.

They bump into me on purpose in the hallway, hissing, "Big Bird." When I try to ignore them, Sloane grabs my arm so hard her nails cut into my skin. "Everyone *hates* you!" she snaps.

"Back off!" says Kate Reeder, who's standing behind us. "Unless you want to get written up for peer counseling."

Sloane practically growls at her, but she slinks away.

"That girl is a total psycho," says Kate. "She's in my study hall, not that she ever shows up. She's got senior early dismissal. So, what are you wearing to prom?"

"I don't know yet," I tell her. "This all just happened."

Kate nods. "Want to go to the mall after school some afternoon? My sister works at one of the boutiques, and she's a total fashionista."

"That sounds really fun," I tell her. I haven't gone shopping with a friend since Valerie moved away. Rachel was never much of a shopper, and in my invisible period, neither was I. But Kate's offer puts me in a much better mood. So does seeing Travis at the end of the day, before he gets changed for track practice. He gives me a hug and quick kiss on the cheek. I walk away feeling the warmth of his lips from one end of the hall to the other.

When I get to my locker, I see that something's been stuck through the slot. I open it carefully. There's a note card impaled on a fish hook.

Q: WHAT DO BIG BIRDS EAT?

I brace myself to find something disgusting, but that's all there is. That's pretty weird, but okay. I head out to my car.

The first thing I see is the letter *A*, written in red lipstick across the windshield. Then I look inside. The front seat is covered with a mound of dirt, which is gross enough, but then I see something moving inside it. I stifle a scream.

Night crawlers. The fat pink worms slither over each other, covered with dirt, and a pile of dead minnows spills over the floor. Someone's been to the live-bait shop.

Someone who has to be Sloane. Kate is right. She's a psycho.

And there she is now, in her car next to Megan and Amber. I wish they didn't see me cringing in disgust, but they do. The three of them are laughing at what must be my horrified expression. Honking, they swoop by so close I have to jump away.

I can feel a familiar heat rising, the spike of a headache behind my right eye. I visualize Sloane's car bursting into flames, and have to forcibly rein in my imagination. I don't want to kill them, just do something witchy. Like . . .

I lift my hands onto my hips and stare straight at Sloane's muffler. Blue smoke pours out with a rattle and roar, and the muffler falls onto the pavement, clanking and sending up sparks. The car draws to an abrupt halt and I hear Sloane's shriek of frustration. It's so satisfying I barely feel guilty for breaking my promise to Rem.

Oops, I think, feeling victorious. *You picked the wrong girl to mess with.*

It's three days till prom night, and I'm at the upscale dress shop where Kate's sister works. I've already tried on a pile of potential prom gowns in my usual color scheme — blue, cream, and silver — and nothing's hit quite the right note. The whole school is still gossiping about my transformation from geeky wallflower to Travis Brown's prom date. Especially since I'm still a junior. All eyes will be on me, and my newfound and still fragile self-confidence won't allow me to walk through the doors of the Harbor Resort looking anything less than my best.

"I liked that white crepe one," says Kate. "It made you look —"

"Pasty," I tell her. "Undead."

"What about this?" asks Kate's sister Hannah. She holds up a gown that my pre-witch self wouldn't have worn on a bet: a flame-colored satin strapless with a scatter of gold bugle beads on the bodice.

"Whoa!" Kate says. "That one is smoking."

"Maybe on you," I say. Kate and Hannah are both curvy, curly-haired brunettes.

"Try it," says Hannah. "I just have a feeling."

I shrug and head back to the louvered fitting room. Its mirror is covered with discarded gowns; I ran out of hook space. The dress seems about the right size as I zip myself in.

Holding my breath, I step into the hallway. I'm looking at three of myself, reflected in three full-length mirrors, and I don't recognize any of them.

Who is that stunning young woman?

The persimmon gown fits me as if it were made with my body in mind. Swathed in bright satin, with my shoulders bare, I look magically gorgeous, my height, wild hair, and ivory skin striking instead of just pale. And there's definitely a wider gold streak in my left eye that makes me look still more exotic.

"Wow," Hannah says, and Kate echoes her. *"Wow!"*

I twirl barefoot in front of the mirror, feeling not just pretty, but powerful. I'll take it.

Hannah fits me out with a gold hair clip and dangly gold earrings, and sends us next door to a shoe store. Kate turns out to wear the same shoe size as me, and we have a blast trying on absurdly high platforms, stilettos, and jaguar-print pumps just for kicks. This is so *prommy*.

"I don't get to do this till next year," Kate says as she teeters in backless pink platforms. "I'm living vicariously."

"There'll be other juniors there."

"Yes," says Kate. "With their drop-dead senior dates."

I can't help smiling. Kate points at the strappy gold sandals I'm wearing.

"Those are the ones. Are they comfortable?"

They actually are, considering I almost never wear heels. I nod.

"All right, then," says Kate. "Next stop, makeovers and mani-pedis."

There may be something more relaxing than lying in a cushioned chair with a warm washcloth over your eyes while your feet and hands bubble in scented spa tubs, but I haven't found it. It's also delicious to share the fun experience with Kate. I still feel unsettled about what happened with Rachel — we've barely spoken since she blew up at me — and as the manicurist paints on a shimmery polish, my mind drifts to wondering whether she's going to prom.

I find out soon enough. After I walk Kate back to her sister's store and pick up my magnificent gown, I run smack into Rachel and Vijay, who's holding a tuxedo rental bag. I wonder if they're going out now, or are still just friends. It gives me a pang that I don't even know.

I've got my hair gathered in the gold clip so it tumbles down one side of my head, showing off my nearly shoulder-length new earrings. My nails are gleaming, and I'm wearing professionally applied eye shadow, blush, and lipstick. Although I'm still in my jeans and T-shirt, I'm also test-driving my strappy gold sandals, so my feet have a chance to get used to the extra three inches.

Rachel looks me up and down. "What *happened* to you?" she asks, shaking her head. Her tone sounds judgmental, and I start to bristle, but then she says, "You look sensational."

"You, too," I say, very relieved. "Have you picked out your prom dress?"

Rachel nods, blushing a little.

"She's going to look incredible," says Vijay, giving Rachel's hand a quick squeeze. So they are going out. I'm so glad. He's really nice, and *almost* as smart as she is. It's great to see Rachel looking so happy. She doesn't seem mad at me anymore, either — maybe a bit wary, but hopefully that will fade fast. I realize how much I've missed being friends with her.

I say good-bye to Rachel and Vijay — telling Rachel I'll call her soon, and meaning it — and head to my car.

I drive back home feeling glowy. After Sloane's little "gift" last week, I took the car to the detailer, who managed to get out the fish smell as well as the dirt. Now the car is so clean I can smell the perfume sample sprayed on my wrist. The moon's coming up, and I note with a pang that it's nearly full. It looks unnaturally large and orange as it hovers above the horizon like some kind of spacecraft. The back road is deserted, and on a dark stretch between hills, my headlights sweep across a lone hitchhiker standing on the shoulder. He's wearing a long black coat.

My blood runs cold as I recognize him. It's the tall, long-haired man I saw near Rem's tugboat and then on Gallows Hill — the one Rem called the earth witch.

I speed past him without stopping, but in the next instant, he's appeared beside me in my passenger seat. I let out a scream of sheer terror, and practically swerve off the road.

"Get out!" I shriek. The steering wheel jerks back under my hands, as if someone else is controlling it. My heart bangs against my rib cage as I realize:

Someone else is.

What is he planning to do to me? I'll fight back. I won't let him.

The car's driving faster and faster. My foot on the brake makes no difference at all. *No wonder Rem is so frightened of him*, I think.

The earth witch's low voice booms with scorn. "Forget about Rem. You're worth twenty of him." My throat goes dry as I realize that he can hear my thoughts.

The moonlight illuminates his craggy features, the rust-colored streak in one inky black eye. He fixes his hypnotic gaze on me.

"Summer solstice is coming," he intones in that cavernous voice. "The moon will be full, and the circle will meet to gather the storm. Salem must pay for its sins."

"Sins?" I echo. Why am I even responding to this creepy phantom? My heart's pounding out of control. "If the people they hanged really *were* witches —"

He cuts off my words. "They were innocent until they were murdered. Our powers took root in the afterlife. Our ancestors' souls were so wronged that the ancient creators — what your world calls witches — granted them magical powers that would bear fruit in the next generations. Some of those families died out; some squandered their magic. And some have been gathering strength for three hundred years."

"What about Sarah Good's curse? And the spell book I found?"

He snorts. "Deranged scribblings from a cracked mind. Did you really think lighting some candles and grinding herb tea could make magic?"

"It did," I say stubbornly.

He shakes his head. "*You* did. The book was a stage prop, an inducement to practice the craft that's within you. None of those spells would have worked without your powers, Abigail. If someone else mixed the same powders and said the same chants, nothing would happen. You have the deep gift, the fire in your veins." His voice rumbles like thunder deep inside a cave. "We've been waiting for you to step forward and join us for centuries."

"What if I don't want to join you?" I hear myself saying. Why are the thoughts in my head coming out of my mouth? I didn't want him to hear me say that.

"You don't have a choice," he answers sternly. "It's why you were sent to us, why you were given these powers. You will meet us on Gallows Hill the night of June twenty-first."

And he's gone, so fast I can practically see him dissolve into the night air. The car nearly spins off the road, but I will it to straighten. He's right. It's my own power that makes these things happen, not words from a book.

My whole body lurches with fright. *Forget Gallows Hill*, I think, gripping the wheel as I drive even faster. *I'll be at the prom.*

Chapter 16

MY HEART'S POUNDING LIKE A DRUM AS I stand in my bedroom, wearing my robe. The prom starts at seven, but Travis is picking me up at six thirty. I've left myself plenty of time to get ready, but everything's taking me longer than I think it should. I'm not used to arranging my unruly hair with a jewelry clip, and the whole new palette of blush and eye shadow I bought from the make-over specialist looks so extreme in my mirror that I wipe it off and redo it three times.

There are other things making me anxious as well, but I'm not going to let them take over my mind. June 21 is Ipswich High prom night. That's all it is. There is no secret circle taking place on Gallows Hill, no dark magic gathering under a rising full moon. I'm just nervous because I've got a really hot date. I'm going with Travis, my crush. End of story.

I take the gown off its hook on the back of my closet door. I run my hand over the flame-colored satin, admiring the beadwork. It is truly gorgeous, but it looks like it belongs on *Dancing with the Stars*, not on me. The Abigail Silva who lurked in the background for so many years isn't quite gone from my psyche. Can I really pull this off? For one anxious moment I think about calling up Travis and telling him this was a giant mistake. He's not really in love with me; he just thinks he is since he's under a spell from a love potion I mixed with my fire-witch powers.

Yeah, right. That'll land me a stretch in the loony bin. I've chosen this path, I've embarked, and there's nothing to do but be bold and hold on for the ride.

I pull the dress over my head and zip it up, holding my breath as it nips in my waist and hugs my torso, giving me curves where I've never had them. Then I put on my long dangly earrings, slip on my gold high-heeled sandals, and take a step back for the full effect.

The girl who stares back from the mirror is unrecognizable, spellbinding. So why do I still feel like awkward old me?

I wonder if celebrities get this feeling as they're about to step out of a limo and walk the red carpet. I wonder if something inside them thinks: *Who am I kidding? It's all just a costume.*

I wish I could cast a spell to calm myself down. But the last thing I want to be doing tonight is anything magical. I'm keeping my distance from Gallows Hill, and the whole town of Salem.

Just then I hear the sound of a car pulling up at the curb. I hurry to the window, pull back my curtain, and watch as Travis bends toward his convertible's mirror to check his hair. As he gets out, he straightens the jacket of his rented tuxedo, adjusting the hem and rechecking his cuff links. This little bit of self-consciousness makes me smile and relax. He may be the idol of Ipswich High School, but he's still just a guy wondering whether he looks all right.

A moment later, I hear the doorbell ring and Dad pulling open the door.

"Abby!" Dad calls up the stairs. "Your date's here!"

Words I never would have imagined I'd hear.

"I'm coming," I call back. I take a deep breath and step out of my room. When I get to the top of the stairs, I see Travis framed in the doorway, looking handsomer than ever in his classic tuxedo and bow tie. I stare down at him as he stares up at me, and the look on his face is pure adoration.

"Whoa!" he breathes. Dad turns to look at me, too,

and I see something in his eyes I've never seen before: pride. It's as if he just noticed me for the first time.

Danielle, at his side, exclaims, "Don't you look beautiful! Doesn't she, Joe?"

"Yes, she does," says Dad, his voice full of wonder and yearning. I know without having to ask that he's thinking of Mom, how much she would have loved being here for this moment, or maybe it's how much I look like her.

I start down the steps, holding my long skirt up. I'm feeling a little like royalty and more than a little like someone who might trip and fall any minute. Travis turns to my dad and shakes hands. Dad introduces Danielle, and we stand in a square, a bit awkwardly, new couple facing new couple.

"Nice car," says Dad. "That's a real classic."

"Thanks," Travis says, and then adds, "I'll drive carefully, sir."

That "sir" is so sweet and old-fashioned, I can't help but smile.

"You better," says Dad. "Precious cargo."

Travis nods and says, "Abby's amazing." He sounds so sincere I feel newly guilty for putting a spell on him. He really is a nice guy. And he's got a terrific smile. I can feel my blush rising, and wonder if it can be seen through the rouge I've brushed on. I might be as red as an apple.

"Do you have a jacket or something?" Travis asks me. "It's a nice night, but you might get cold with the top down. Or I could put it up, so your hair won't get messed up. Whatever you'd like."

He's so eager to please me. Would Rem have thought of those details? Doubtful. He'd probably want us to go to the prom in a kayak.

"Top down sounds great," I say. "Thanks."

I can picture us driving along the coast road with the wind in our hair and the sky overhead, and it sounds like heaven. But I hadn't thought of a jacket. I rack my brains. What in the world do I own that won't look completely insane with an orange strapless prom gown? I've got several hoodies, a pea coat, and a jean jacket. No, no, and no.

Danielle sees my look of distress and says, "I've got something I think might be perfect." She goes to the closet and takes out an elegant shawl, a coppery raw silk that will go just as well with my gown as it does with her auburn hair. "How about this?" she offers. "I've had it dry-cleaned, so it won't smell like smoke."

"It's gorgeous," I breathe. "Is that really all right?"

"I'd be delighted," Danielle says. She actually sounds like she means it, which makes it feel almost all right that she's keeping clothes in our closet. She drapes the shawl over my shoulders, adjusting it. "Now can we take some pictures? You're *such* a cute couple."

You know what? We are. So why does my heart feel so hollow as we stand and pose side by side?

I brush the feeling away, flashing a smile as Dad frames us both with his camera. This is my dream night. And I'm going to enjoy every minute, so there.

The prom's theme is "Enchanted Evening," and it's being held at the Beverly Harbor Resort, a seaside hotel with a wraparound deck overlooking the ocean. Salem is just a few miles away, on the opposite side of the bay, but this feels like a different world. The hotel is all modern and sleek, and the low-slanting sun makes its windows look like burnished gold. It's the longest twilight of the year, with a few wisps of clouds striping the sky over rippling white dunes and a sea filled with glittering highlights. Enchanted evening, indeed.

Travis gets out of the car and circles around it to open my door. His walk is so easy and confident, and he looks like a movie star in that tuxedo. He offers his hand as I rise, and I take it gratefully. With my new heels on, we're practically eye to eye.

"You look awesome," he says, and I can't help smiling. All the years I've had a long-distance crush on this guy, and he's standing inches away from me, telling me that I look awesome. I soak it in, trying to push away any stray thoughts about Gallows Hill, spell books, or potions.

"You, too, Travis. Thanks." But he doesn't let go of my hand. He just stands there staring at me like he can't believe what he's seeing. "What is it?"

"Your eyes. I never noticed that they were two colors."

I try to smile, feeling self-conscious. *That's the sign*, Rem had told me. "My brother says they look like marbles."

"Your brother is nuts," he says, grinning. "They look like they have stars in them. Actual stars. Are you ready?"

I nod, and we set out for the hotel arm in arm. I can see couples in formal wear out on the deck, and a few other cars pulling in, but they fade into the background. It's all about me and my date.

No wonder I seem to have stars in my eyes.

I take a deep breath as we cross the parking lot. I can smell salt air and wild beach roses, the perfume of summer. The breakers roll up on the shore in their ancient rhythm, and the sky shimmers.

When we reach the entry, a doorman pulls open the heavy glass door, smiling at us. The hotel lobby is covered with twinkle lights. Everything's perfect . . . or nearly. As I take a step over the threshold, I have a sudden vision of furniture flying, shrieks, chaos. It hits with the sudden force of one of my spike headaches, stabbing into my brain like an ice pick.

And then it's gone, so suddenly it seems unreal. I shake it off with a shiver, clutching Travis's hand as we go inside.

Unfortunately, the first person I see, after we cross the lobby and enter the ballroom, is Megan. She's wearing a shell-pink sheath that fits her like a slice of ham. With her dark hair piled high on her head and cream-colored stilettos, she looks very much like a Kardashian sister. But my eyes go right to her throat. She's wearing the crystal pendant I sold her at Spiral Visions, but she's hung the heart upside down.

"Like it, Abby?" she says. "*You're* the reason I decided to wear it upside down. Because *some* people have it all upside down. Hi, Travis."

And off she sweeps, with some muscle-bound guy from the football team who she's commandeered as her date.

Travis only shakes his head, as if Megan is just embarrassing herself, and takes my elbow as we keep walking.

Amber and Sloane are here, too, in floral-print mermaid gowns they must have bought at the same clearance sale. Both of them glare at me like I'm a criminal. From the way their heads lean together, I'm certain they're plotting some kind of revenge.

Well, let them. If push comes to shove, I'm sure I can top it.

The dance floor is already crowded. There's a live band playing a loud rock song on the opposite side of the room, and a mirror ball twirling above. Seniors I've never seen outside of gym class or Spanish are dancing in pairs, dressed in rented tuxedos and gowns from the mall. There are enough sequins to gild a parade float. I spot Rachel, in a demure but flattering royal blue gown, dancing with Vijay, whose glasses are crooked. I wave, but they don't see me. They look like they're having a wonderful time.

Several teachers are acting as chaperones, and they're dressed up, too, which is very bizarre to see. Ms. Baptiste wears a maroon velvet evening gown. My geeky biology teacher, Dr. Aran, is stationed right next to the punch bowl, wearing a lavender tux that he probably bought for his own prom sometime in the '80s. I wonder if he had a mullet.

"Can I get you something to drink?" Travis asks. The music is so loud he's practically shouting.

I nod and yell back to him, "Thanks."

He gets into the punch bowl line next to some of his track team buddies, and I watch them jostle and tease, trading good-natured jokes about bow ties and cummerbunds. People are filling their plates at a long buffet table along one wall, heaped with platters of veggies and dip, cheese and crackers, and big chafing dishes of fried ravioli and buffalo wings. I'm suddenly hungry. I was too nervous to touch Danielle's dinner.

A few white-jacketed waiters circulate, passing trays of miniature quiches, crab cakes, and spring rolls. One of the waiters brushes against my shoulder. I reach for a crab cake and nearly choke: the cater-waiter is Rem!

"You have to get out of here, *now*," he hisses. "They're here."

"Who?" I say. I'm so stunned to see him it's hard to form words. "Why are *you* here?"

"I had to warn you. Please, Abby. You need to get out now, before it's too late."

Why does he have to look at me like that? Those eyes sear right into my soul. The connection between us is like being hit by heat lightning.

Ms. Baptiste takes a crab cake from Rem's tray. Another waitstaffer, a stocky woman with dark, heavy hair twisted into a bun, steps forward, shooting Rem a fierce look of warning. I guess she's his boss, but there seems to be something more going on. The back of my neck prickles, but I decide to ignore it — and Rem.

Or try to, at least. Knowing that he's in the same room makes it all but impossible to think of anything else. My heart's beating faster than usual, and I'm hugely relieved when Travis comes back with two punch cups. I gulp mine down quickly and ask him if he'd like to dance.

"Sure," he grins. "That's what we're here for, right?" He sets our punch cups aside and walks me out onto the dance floor.

But dancing is the absolute wrong way to clear my head. All I can think of is doing the Dougie with Rem, ankle-deep in the water of our secret cove, and that sublime moment when he picked me up in his arms. Travis is cute and sweet, and he couldn't be any more doting — I made sure of that — but that one lightning-bolt look between me and Rem is all it takes for me to realize that I've been kidding myself. I could no more forget about him than I could forget my own name. He's a part of me. I'm a part of him. It's that simple.

And he didn't reject me, not really. Whatever Rem did to push me away was meant to keep me from succumbing to the witch's kiss, when the earth witch was pulling his strings like a puppet. He did it because he loves me, and what did I do? Turned around and used magic to gain another boy's love.

Travis holds me tighter against his chest, and I feel like a traitor. We're moving closer and closer to the bandstand, as if something is drawing us in that direction. I feel an electrical crackle around me. The air starts to shimmer, and I feel light-headed. Is it from dancing with Travis, or knowing that Rem's right across the room?

I close my eyes, hoping to get lost in the music and shake off this dizzy uneasiness. When I open my eyes again, we've reached the edge of the stage. For the first time, I have a clear view of the band — in fact, I'm looking right at the drummer. He's louche and tattooed, with a scarf tied around his lank hair and one dangling earring. As he moves his limbs, rattling hi-hats and brushing the snare drum, the stage lights catch a telltale streak of red in his left eye.

My breath seems to freeze in my lungs.

It's the earth witch.

He's looking at me with a sardonic smirk, and I hear his deep voice echo inside my head: *I told you we'd see you tonight.*

Now I'm really terrified. The prom is infested with witches! If he's earth, Rem's water, and I'm fire, the only branch missing is air . . . on the full-moon solstice night when it's been prophesied that all four elements will come together to take vengeance on Salem. I didn't go to Gallows Hill, but it came to me.

No wonder Rem told me I had to get out.

My head's pounding as if it's about to explode. I feel dizzy and feverish, and I'm breaking out in a sweat.

"I've got to go to the ladies' room," I tell Travis, and bolt from the crowded dance floor.

I zigzag between moving bodies, trying to force my way through. As I pass the buffet table, I overhear the catering captain chastising Rem.

"You're not the only water witch here," she snaps. "We can manage without you. It's *her* we need. Fire." She meets my eye, and I realize one of her dark eyes is dappled with green. And that I have seen her before: She's that other inspector from the RMV. The one Rem said had sent me to Salem. I even remember her name: Esperanza. And, of course, she's also a witch.

This is getting worse every minute. If I had my car keys, I'd speed away like a bullet. But I came in Travis's car, so I'm trapped. There's nothing outside except sand dunes and pavement. There's no place to hide. I stumble into the ladies' room just off the lobby.

It's a suite, with brocade benches and a mirrored wall

in the powder room. Before I can catch my breath, I spot three figures in the mirror: Megan, Amber, and Sloane. They've been waiting behind the door. I turn around to dash back out, but Amber and Sloane each grab one of my arms, twisting them savagely behind my back so that any move I make will hurt me. I let out a scream but the music outside is much louder.

Megan steps forward. "You think you can just help yourself to my boyfriend?" she asks, reaching into her purse for a can of black spray paint. She presses the nozzle, zigzagging it over my gown. I try to jerk away but it's no use — the girls are holding me firmly. In seconds, my gown is splattered with black paint and I'm too stunned to shout or cry.

"Let's see how Travis likes your dress now," Megan hisses.

"Oh, she looks so cute," sneers Amber.

"Smoking," says Sloane.

Megan finishes spraying and drops the can into the trash. I see something gleam in the mirror, and realize that Sloane is holding a pair of scissors. I feel a hot surge of panic. Is she going to stab me?

"Somebody needs a new haircut," Sloane sneers, removing my hair clip and tossing it onto the floor. She grabs hold of a clump of my hair and slices it close to my scalp. I don't dare to struggle; the scissors are too close to my face. She lops off several more chunks at odd angles, dropping them onto the carpet. Her beady eyes gleam. I want to throw up.

"You look hideous," Megan tells me. "It suits you."

"Enjoy the prom, loser!" Amber shrieks in shrill tones, and the three of them rush from the bathroom in fits of hysterical laughter.

The whole thing happened so fast that I had no time to react. Now I look at myself in the mirror and burst into sobs. My hair is in uneven tufts and my whole scalp is burning. I look like a freak show. There's paint on my arms and my gown is graffitied with large black splotches.

As the tears fall and I hug myself in horror, I wonder: How could I let Megan do this to me? Why didn't I torch her pink prom gown, set fire to her hair?

So much for my being a powerful witch. When it comes right down to the crunch, I'm nothing but a scared teenage girl. For the first time, I actually wish that I had crossed over, so I could come into my full fiery strength.

I feel a rumbling deep under my feet, like an earthquake. There's a sudden explosion of splintering wood and cracked tiles in the bathroom. One of the stall doors slams open with hurricane force, revealing a broken back wall.

Framed amid the rubble is an upright, strong older woman, dressed in what looks like an ancient black robe. It takes me a moment to recognize my great-aunt Gail.

When I do, my heart pounds as the realization drops into place: She is the air witch, backlit by the rising full moon.

"It's time," she says, seizing my hand between her bony fingers. "Time to take your revenge."

Before I can blink, Gail and I have materialized in the center of the dance floor. She holds my right hand in an iron grip as I take in the terrifying scene before me.

The prom is in swirling chaos. Girls shriek and cover their heads as napkins and tablecloths fly through the air. Chairs and buffet trays fly upward, and the walls tremble. It's like an indoor tornado. Outside the windows, a violent sea storm has blown up out of nowhere. Thunder and lightning crash through blackening skies, and a howling wind lashes gray waves into froth.

The curtain rods over the windows give way, crashing down like the mast of a sinking ship. A loose beam swings down from the ceiling. People scream and stampede for the door, but it's already blocked by piles of debris. As I watch in horror, a round table teeters onto its edge and starts rolling drunkenly over the floor. Couples cling to each other as hors d'oeuvres, forks, and punch cups fly past them.

I see Samson Hobby grab hold of a passing beef slider, popping it into his mouth. For one crazy second, I want to laugh, and then Samson gets hit by a flying chair. Everyone's screaming.

The loudest screams come from Megan, Amber, and Sloane, who cower on the floor in terror as a circle of knives swirl over their heads. Freaked out as I am, it gives me a grim satisfaction to watch them snivel and cringe. If I knew a spell to make those knives cut their hair off, I'd do it. My raw scalp still burns, and as I reach my free hand up to cover the ugly tufts, I remember the splotches of paint on my dress. I don't want Rem or Travis to see me like this, but it isn't just shame that floods through me. It's a pure, boiling fury. I want those girls to pay.

The mirror ball falls from the ceiling and crashes in glittering shards right by Amber, Megan, and Sloane. The lights on the dance floor start flashing bloodred. Suddenly, the earth witch drummer and Esperanza materialize before me and Gail. The water and earth witch are clasping each other's hands with a grip like cement. As Gail takes Esperanza's hand, a plume of steam hisses upward from the floor. The three older witches chant an incantation:

"*Earth, air, water, fire,*

On this night,
What was wrong shall be made right . . ."

Gail holds my right hand in a vise-like grip, dragging me into the circle, but I keep my left hand on top of my head. I can't bring myself to clasp hands with that sinister earth witch.

He fixes his red-streaked eye on me, chanting louder. *"Earth, air, water, fire . . ."*

My head starts to throb. My left hand is pulled down from my head and toward his by a magnetic force, so powerful it threatens to rip my arm out of its socket. I remember Rem's words — *he can make me do things I don't want to do* — and force my hand back down to my side. Where is Rem now? Was he hurt? I look around wildly.

"I told you the child wasn't ready!" Gail hisses to the others.

"Yes, she is." The earth witch's eyes bore into mine. "Your power is boiling inside, rising through you like lava. I can taste your rage. Let it erupt."

I feel his strength pulling at me like quicksand, and Gail's is flowing down my right arm with hurricane force. Esperanza's hair has come loose and it ripples like snakes in black water. I can't resist so much power. Drawn into the vortex, my left hand starts to rise by itself. My fingers touch the earth witch's and I feel them lock, twisting together like tree roots. My hand starts to melt into his, an alchemical fusion, the four of us welding together into a single unholy fused circle, like points of a compass.

And then I see Travis, staring at me in stunned disappointment, as if he can't believe this is who I am. Right behind him are Rachel and Vijay, who's been knocked to the floor. His glasses are gone and there's blood on his forehead. Rachel is sobbing and trying to comfort him. Samson Hobby's out cold.

What will happen to all these innocent people? Isn't this random destruction far worse than killing those twenty people in Salem all those years ago? Any revenge wrought on Salem tonight won't do a thing to Nicholas Noyes and the magistrates who ordered the hangings, or the citizens who gave false evidence and spread vicious rumors, or anyone else from that long-ago time. The storm raging outside will rain down on the people who live in Salem right now, on Dyami and Ugly Gus and the shopkeepers I've come to care for. No matter how much I might long for revenge against Megan and her awful friends, I'm still much too human to join in this evil.

Summoning every shred of my strength, I take a step backward. A searing pain throbs through my hand, as if all the flesh has been torn off my palm. There's a wave of volcanic heat and acrid black smoke. Someone grabs my free elbow — Rem, who's battled his way through the panicked crowd. The earth witch snarls as Rem pulls me away from the witches' circle. His eye pulses bloodred.

As Rem and I try to escape through the chaos, my feet are jerked out from under me. Rem and I are lifted right off the floor. The earth witch must have cast a spell that sends both of us tumbling through the air like a pair of sock puppets. When we land again, hard, my left hand sears like lava. The ground shakes and rumbles, and I feel the floor cracking open beneath us. For the first time tonight, I wonder if I might die. I'm shaking with terror.

Rem turns to face me, his hand on my shoulder. "Kiss me."

"What?" Has he lost his mind? That's the worst thing we could do! "But the witch's kiss —"

"Now. With your full human heart." He takes me in his arms, bringing his beautiful face so close to mine that we're breathing each other's breath. I feel his warm lips open against mine, and I kiss him with every ounce of emotion I have. Even the pain in my hand is forgotten. What I feel flowing between us is nothing but plain, unadorned love — the kind that has nothing to do with spells.

There is nothing I don't want to give to Rem; I'm his, and he's mine. With a huge clap like thunder, the room shakes, and everything seems to go black.

When my eyes open, I'm covered in sand. I shift and feel its gritty wetness beneath me, the scrape of beach grass and shell fragments. I'm on the dunes. There's sand in my mouth and in my long, tangled hair.

Hair. I have hair again.

I blink my eyes, and feel something shifting beside me. It's Rem, also covered with sand. Somehow we've been hurled outside, onto the beach.

"What just happened?" I breathe, feeling sand grit on my tongue.

He shakes his head, and I realize he doesn't know any more than I do. But we're both alive. The waves roll and crash in a steady, majestic roar. There are stars overhead in the calm sky. There's no storm.

I reach up to touch my hair. It's all back, wild as ever. But the palm of my left hand is still raw and blistered.

I didn't imagine it.

"Rem?" I ask, fearful.

He rolls onto his side and I notice his white shirt is ripped. He looks at my livid-red hand and winces in sympathy. "We'll have to take care of that."

"You kissed me," I say, remembering. He nods. "I thought if you kissed me, your power would go —"

"To the stronger energy. Your human self won."

Rem smiles at me, and I realize both of his eyes are completely green. No more wedge of bright blue. They still make me breathless, though. "Did you know that would happen?" I ask.

He shakes his head. "Not till I saw you step back from the circle. And not even then. I took a chance."

"But what if I hadn't —"

"You did, Abby. Somehow you found the strength to defy all that evil. All by yourself, you reversed the storm."

"I don't understand. What happened to everyone — ?"

"Shhhh. Do you hear that?" Rem holds up his finger. The sound of the surf is so loud that it seems to drown everything else out. Then I hear it, too. Somewhere behind us, music is playing.

We look at each other, then get up and dust off our clothing. My gown is no longer spray-painted. Except for the stray grains of sand in the beadwork, it's just as it was.

Rem has started to walk toward the music. My high heels dig into the sand, and I slip off both gold sandals and carry them in my right hand. The left is still throbbing.

We clamber up over the edge of the dune, and we're next to the parking lot of the Beverly Harbor Resort. The evening is balmy and the prom is in full swing inside the hotel. Rem and I look at each other again, in silent wonder.

I take a few steps toward the wraparound deck. Looking in through the windows, I can see that the curtains and tables are all back in place. Travis is dancing with Megan, who looks giddy — and is wearing her heart necklace right side up. Amber and Sloane are huddled by the punch bowl, looking as miserable in their own cruelty as ever they did. Vijay is spinning Rachel around the dance floor. A red-headed waiter is passing Ms. Baptiste a crab cake . . . and the band's drummer is a girl.

Great-aunt Gail, Esperanza, and the earth witch are nowhere in sight. The mirror ball spins, sending sparkles of light through the air.

Rem steps up behind me, placing one hand on my shoulder. I turn toward him, eyes wide. "I don't get it. How did everything get back to normal?"

"You broke the circle. Our kiss broke the spell." I must still look blank, because he goes on. "Elemental magic is a powerful force. It can cut across time and space. That's how the earth witch sent us to Gallows Hill that day, how your great-aunt got here from the nursing home."

"And why she seemed younger?"

Rem nods. "When all four elements fuse, it's more powerful still. But you renounced your fire, and sent time spinning backward. To everyone inside, the storm never happened."

"So everything goes back to — ?"

"What should have been. What was meant to be." Rem raises a hand to my face. As he strokes my cheek, I look into his eyes, realizing there's still a faint shadow of blue in the vivid green. He hasn't lost every bit of his magic. That must mean I haven't as well.

"Speaking of meant to be . . ." Rem's dimples appear. He gathers me into his arms and kisses me under the rising full moon.

Chapter 17

THE CLEAR BLUE SKY ARCHES ABOVE AS THE whole senior class sits in rows of folding chairs on the football field. They're all wearing blue and white graduation robes. The rest of us are spread out on tiered bleachers, listening to Rachel's valedictorian speech.

The topic she chose was "Potential." She stands at the podium, speaking without any notes (how Rachel is that?) about all the gifts everybody is born with, and the different experiences that can help them to flower. Even experiences of pain and loss and what seem at the time like mistakes.

As she speaks, I think of the many mistakes I've made. Though my nightmares and headaches have vanished along with my magical powers, I can't shake the images of that awful storm at the prom — the storm no one except me and Rem will ever remember. *Because of me*, I think with some pride. *I'm the one who sent time spinning back-ward and rescued everyone at prom — and in Salem.*

We're all better off with the remixed version of June 21. Even my great-aunt Gail, whose stroke-ravaged body apparently took its last breath that night. I hope her spirit is finally at peace.

Esperanza, it seems, has returned to her day job at the RMV. Nobody knows what became of the aging rock drummer with one mangled hand who was briefly spotted lurking around Salem. But I hope that I'll never see him again.

"It's like gardening," Rachel is saying now, and I focus back on her. "Some plants need dry soil and others need rain or a long snowy winter. What was dormant in one season may burst into bloom in another. The same thing is true for ourselves. Sometimes our growth comes from hard work and diligence. Sometimes it's the sunshine of friendship."

She scans the crowd, finding me in the sea of faces. I smile at her, touched.

As Rachel goes on with her speech, my mind wanders over my own strange gifts that I discovered were lying dormant. Is there something good that can blossom from magical powers, some extra sparkling of the soul that not everyone gets, like being born with perfect pitch or a talent for dance? It's not just a question of what gifts you're given, but how you choose to use them, what shoes you put on to move forward in life. Revenge is a terrible thing, but the world needs a sprinkling of magic.

And that's what I seem to have left. Just a sprinkling, like cinnamon on a cappuccino.

Rachel finishes up with a quote from Thomas Edison: "If we did the things we are capable of, we would astound ourselves." She looks around at her classmates. "Got that, guys? Let's go and astound ourselves. Congratulations!"

There's a roar of applause and approval. Parents and friends in the bleachers hoot and cheer, rising to their feet for a standing ovation. I jump up, too, but I can't clap. My left hand is still wrapped in gauze, and the blisters are painful, even with the ointment. I've told everyone I got burned, which is sort of the truth.

Kate jumps up beside me. "Rachel was *great*!" she exclaims. "Who knew she was such an incredible public speaker?"

Just one of those gifts that can blossom. I'm sure Rachel will go on to do amazing things. I am so proud of my friend. It took me some time to realize that, just as I feared she would leave me behind when she went off to college, Rachel was scared I would leave her behind when I got a boyfriend. That isn't an issue between us anymore, and not just because she and Vijay are officially dating. It's more that we've learned that our friendship is strong enough to survive the inevitable times when one of us pulls ahead of the other.

The crowd settles back down as the principal hands out diplomas. The long list of names hums along, and I cheer extra loud for Rachel. When the last senior collects his diploma, there's another big cheer, and mortarboard hats fly through the air like confetti.

Kate and I thread our way through the crowd of exuberant graduates. I stop to congratulate Travis, who's posing for cell phone photos with his track team buddies.

"Thanks!" he says, flashing the same generically friendly smile he gives to everyone. Then he adds my name — "Thanks, Abby!" — with what seems like extra warmth. I can't help wondering, as I have throughout this past week, exactly how much of the tape got erased when the spell was reversed at the prom. Does Travis have any memory of us going to look at the lighthouse and kissing? Does he recall eating that magical cupcake I baked for him?

As Rem explained it, the fabric of time folded back not to a specific time or day, but to what *should have been*. And it seems as if some dangling threads go back further than others.

The one thing that didn't go back at all was the wound on my hand. My doctor assured me the skin will regenerate, and that I'll have a full range of motion, but there will be scar tissue. It seems only right that my body should hold a reminder of what could have happened on that fateful night.

Danielle has turned out to be a sympathetic nurse. She told me she also once burned her hand on a cast-iron skillet (that excuse sounded more plausible than molten lava from fusing my palm with the earth witch), and still remembers how much it hurt. She rewraps my gauze bandages carefully every morning and evening, which has given us time to talk — short conversations, but often intense ones. I've found out that her father walked out on her family when she was in high school, leaving her mother for somebody else, and it's taken her years to get over her anger. She's moving back into her own house next week, as soon as the construction is finished, and she's in no hurry to marry my dad. "Men always want to jump into another relationship," she says. "Women know that it takes time."

I nod at these words. It's taken me plenty of time to sort out things with Dad, but lately I've felt that he's starting to pay more attention to me. Matt might be his prize soccer player, but I know Dad and I will always share a special bond when it comes to our vivid memories of Mom. And that's a good thing.

Travis reaches over to pull Megan into the photo. The boy with the cell phone yells out, "Looking *good*, you two!" and Megan laughs, delighted.

I've noticed that since the prom hit the Reset button, Megan has started to seem a bit softer. Maybe it's losing that sharp edge of jealousy, now that Travis is looking at no one but her. Or maybe the spray of blackheads across her once-perfect skin has taught her a bit of humility.

She's also stopped speaking to her former sidekicks. Just frozen them out. They look appropriately lonely and sour right now. I glance over at Amber, who's apparently had laryngitis since prom night — she speaks in a whispery croak, theatrically placing a hand at the base of her throat. Rumor has it the condition might last for months, even years. Meanwhile, Sloane's hair has been cut very ragged and short since it got caught in a ladies' room hand dryer (also on prom night, I've heard). It's not an attractive look on her, and she's desperately yanking on a strand of hair right now, as if willing it to grow faster.

Could I have had something to do with these girls' recent misfortunes? I'm not ruling it out altogether, but I'd like to think it was karma.

Kate is already standing with Rachel, who's flanked by both of her parents and Vijay's huge family. One of his little sisters is climbing his leg, and another is spinning around with his mortarboard hat on her head.

"You were amazing!" I tell Rachel.

She gives me a big hug. "Are you sure you can't come to the pool party at Vijay's?" she asks. "His mother is making a feast. And you won't have to swim. You've got an airtight excuse." She looks at the gauze on my hand. "How's it feeling?"

I lift it up, shrugging. I am healing, bit by bit. "Gets better every day," I say. "It's like magic."

Epilogue

I DRIVE UP THE LONG ARCHING SPAN OF the bridge to Salem, feeling something that still strikes me as a miracle: totally normal. No colorful visions, no spike headaches, no phobias about drowning. I've come a long way.

The hot August sun bakes down on my roof as I drive through the village of Salem, passing all the familiar landmarks. I slow down a bit as I pass the green awning of Spiral Visions, where I still work every weekend, and the Double Double Café, where Kara is sweeping the sidewalk. I'm happy to note that there isn't a parking space anywhere near it.

A bright red trolley bus passes in front of me, ringing its musical bell. It's packed to the gills with tourists. I continue to drive through town, braking for shoppers and moms pushing strollers, and into the quieter section of waterfront streets to the south of the wharf. I drive out past

Salem State College. The houses get farther apart on the outskirts of town. My heart starts to flutter when I reach the parking spot under the willows, near the secluded cove where I had my first swimming lesson.

I pop open the trunk of the Jetta, noticing that my left hand is losing its stiffness. The scar tissue's darker than most of my skin, but that's not saying much.

I shoulder my beach bag and head down the footpath alongside the creek, noting how much fuller and greener the willows have gotten. The small stretch of sandy beach is deserted, but I spot a kayak pulled up next to the flat rock, where there's a sketchbook and paint box. I look at it, smiling. So Rem is already here somewhere. All summer long, he's been working on his portfolio for art school applications — I finally convinced him he might win a scholarship. Talent, after all, is a cousin to magic.

I spread out my striped towel and sit down to wait for him, tipping my face toward the sun. Maybe I'll actually get something that can pass for a tan this summer. That would make for a different start to senior year.

But I have the sense that the differences in me are more than skin deep. They're more about confidence, and feeling closer to people. Especially one person.

Suddenly, I feel something ice cold against my back. It's literally spine-chilling.

Rem has come back bearing two cups of soda. He holds them out, flashing his dimples. "Root beer or ginger ale?"

Laughing, I twist around to grab the root beer cup out of his hand, but I drop it. Quick as a flash, Rem reaches to catch it . . . and misses.

He's got human reflexes now. And that's just fine with me.

The root beer soaks into my towel, but I ignore it, grinning at Rem.

"Come on," I say, jumping up and grabbing his hand. "Let's go swimming."

Acknowledgments

THANKS TO SOPHIA AND RUBY, MY TRAVEL companions in Salem; the Harden family, for local color; Laura Shaine, for keeping the home fires burning; Susan Cohen and Phyllis Wender at the Gersh Agency; and my hardworking coven at Scholastic: Aimee Friedman, Ruth Ames, Becky Shapiro, Yaffa Jaskoll, Jackie Hornberger, Elizabeth Krych, Ed Masessa, Tracy van Straaten, Abby McAden, and David Levithan.

Don't miss a remarkable new novel about troubled ghosts, hidden secrets, and the streets of New Orleans.

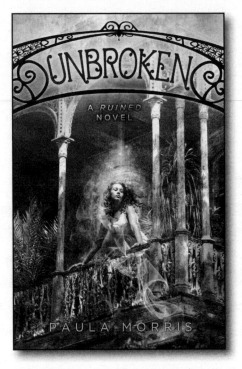

Unbroken: A Ruined Novel
by Paula Morris

Rebecca wriggled into her coat and darted out the red front door. When she looked up, the boy with blue eyes was standing right in front of her, close enough to touch.

"Please," he said. He sounded foreign — British or Irish or something.

"What do you want?" Rebecca hissed, edging toward the restaurant door. Just because he was good-looking didn't mean this guy wasn't dangerous.

"You don't know me," he said, still staring at her, "but I . . . I've seen you before. You were down in New Orleans. I saw you with Lisette."

Something surged through her — a sickening dread, charged with the electric tingle of excitement. This boy knew Lisette. So did this mean he was a ghost, too? No, that was ridiculous. It was impossible.

"I saw you with her," the boy said, a desperate edge to his voice. Rebecca's heart thudded. Nobody could have seen her that day on St. Philip Street, because when Rebecca held Lisette's hand, she disappeared from view. She was invisible, just as Lisette was invisible to other people. They could walk through the crowded streets of the city, unseen and undetected by anyone. Anyone, that is, except other ghosts.

As though he understood what she was looking for, the boy inched back his jacket. His white shirt was stained with a huge dark splotch of what might have been ink, or was more likely blood.